ALSO BY GORDON KORMAN

Son of the Mob

Son of the Mob 2: Hollywood Hustle

Jake, Reinvented

Maxx Comedy

The 6th Grade Nickname Game

I Want to Go Home

No Coins, Please

The *On the Run* series

The *Kidnapped* series

The *Dive* series

The *Everest* series

The *Island* series

The *Macdonald Hall* series

For
LEO FRANCIS KORMAN,
BORN TO ROCK 4/17/05

PROLOGUE

The thing about a cavity search is this: it has nothing to do with the dentist. If only it did.

They can give it polite names, like "additional inspection" or "supplemental investigation." But the fact is, you're bent over, grabbing your ankles, while some total stranger has his fingers in a very private place where nobody should be rummaging around.

Don't get me wrong. It doesn't scar you for life. You don't suffer from post-traumatic stress syndrome. But no one who has been through it is ever quite the same again. The experience is just—*big*.

I'll go even further than that. There are two kinds of people in this world—those who have had a cavity search, and those who haven't. This is the story of how I wound up in the wrong category.

It's the story of other things, too. A cavity search, while excruciatingly memorable, doesn't actually define who you turn out to be. When

I was president of my high school's Young Republicans, accepted to Harvard, and on a fast track to a six-figure income, I believed that we are masters of our own fate. Now I know that just the opposite is probably true. You are the sum of what happens to you, a pinball, bouncing from bumper to bumper, hoping the impact of the flippers won't hurt much. That theory—how I came up with it, anyway—turned out to be all part of my inexorable journey to that little room the Cleveland PD called Exam 3. . . .

[1]

THE TERMS *YOUNG REPUBLICAN* AND *cavity search* don't often appear together. Republicans don't have cavity searches. According to my oldest friend, Melinda Rapaport, we don't even have cavities.

But I wasn't born Republican. It's not genetic. Believe me—I'm familiar with genetics. I have McMurphy, the eight-hundred-pound gorilla I carry in my DNA, a total loose cannon rolling around my personality.

We all have wild impulses from who-knows-where. In my case, I know exactly where. Mine come from McMurphy.

The only connection between genetics and being a Republican is that I joined the G.O.P. to help myself control McMurphy. And even that's not technically true.

The real reason was Congressman DeLuca. It was two summers ago. Gates signed on to help out with DeLuca's re-election campaign—that's Caleb Drew. We called him Gates because he was the next Bill Gates for sure. He brought Fleming Norwood. I only went by campaign headquarters to keep those guys company. The minute I saw Shelby Rostov stuffing envelopes, I was lost. Blond, blue eyes. Not just hot—Shelby was what you always pictured when you envisioned the ideal of hot. The effect was so striking that I almost *recognized* her: *Hey, don't I know you from my wildest dreams?*

I grabbed a pile of envelopes and started stuffing right along with her.

"Fresh blood?" she asked. Her smile was so beamingly bright that I had to keep from squinting.

"The freshest." Boredom had brought me to the G.O.P. Love kept me there.

Congressman DeLuca was the kind of guy who was easy to support. He just seemed so different from other politicians. For starters, he was pretty young—late thirties—with loads of charisma. When he talked about something, you really wanted to believe him. His ideas weren't super-conservative; they were common sense. That was his campaign slogan—The Common Sense Revolution.

The only flak I caught over working for the congressman came from Melinda. To say that she was un-Republican was to understate the matter by one thousand percent. On the outside, she was somewhere between goth and punk, but her gut was pure, unadulterated liberal. Her heart bled for every twig and spotted owl. If there were a People for the Ethical Treatment of Amoebas, she would have joined. To her, there was nothing more despicable in this world than corporate profits—unless the money could be diverted to buy Wite-Out to erase Christopher Columbus from all the history books.

"You joined the *Republicans*? Leo, what's wrong with you?"

"You should meet Congressman DeLuca," I argued. "He's the real deal."

"He's the devil."

"Come on!" I snorted.

"Oh, sorry—the devil is the guy with the pointy tail, plotting for everybody's soul. Like a supernatural being has nothing better to do than obsess over whether or not I pierce my tongue. P.S.—mind control."

"Nobody controls my mind," I defended myself.

"In all the time I've known you," she said

dramatically, "I never thought you'd get suckered in by the Big Lie."

There was no arguing with Melinda when she started a sentence with "In all the time I've known you." Besides my parents, she knew me longer than anyone. We were toddlers together, beating each other over the head with toys while our moms had coffee. As far back as I could go, there had always been a Melinda. She knew everything about me—except McMurphy. I didn't tell anybody about him.

This was Melinda's official response to me working for the G.O.P. She volunteered for DeLuca's opponent. The Democrat? Not on your life. She signed on to stump for a candidate named Vinod Murti. I don't remember the party affiliation, but their only two issues were legalizing marijuana and yogic flying. (Don't ask.)

Vinod ran out of money before Election Day and left the state, sticking his supporters with an eleven-hundred-dollar tab from the local vegan restaurant. Our guy won by a landslide.

I was hooked. Success is a heady business.

Here's an example of the sheer nerve of Melinda. She actually expected me to bring her along on the victory party cruise that Congressman DeLuca threw for his campaign staff.

"Absolutely not!" I told her. "You worked for his opponent. Go on *his* cruise—maybe he's got a rowboat."

Yet even as I was arguing, I knew exactly how it was going to turn out. She was going, and I was taking her. Period. There were no threats, no bribes. She simply refused to accept that it wasn't going to happen. And it happened.

She was already pretty punked out by then, so she stood out like a sore thumb.

The cruise was a nightmare. Gates couldn't take his eyes off her, as if a rare exotic monkey had somehow found its way onto our boat trip. She bad-mouthed the congressman from bow to stern and back again. She got into a beef with Fleming about her spiderweb tattoo, and wound up giving him the finger in front of half the Connecticut G.O.P.

"Is that your girlfriend, Leo?" Shelby asked in awe.

I tried to laugh it off. "God forbid!"

"But you guys came together, right?"

What could I do? Deny it?

"Old friends," I mumbled. "Like from the Cretaceous period."

Later that night I saw Shelby making out with Fleming on the poop deck. If I'd known that getting flipped off by a goth-punk was such an endorsement in her eyes, I'd have made a deal with Melinda to punch me.

As parties went, it wasn't my favorite. Still, that was the night Representative DeLuca offered to be our sponsor for a chapter of the Young Republicans at East Brickfield Township High School. At that moment, in the glow of his election victory, we would have followed the guy over the rail into the chilly waters of the Long Island Sound. We were sold.

Funny thing—throughout the whole ride, I moved heaven and earth to steer Melinda away from the congressman. It made sense, right? The distinguished gentleman from Connecticut shouldn't have to be abused on his own boat trip. But when their paths inevitably did cross that night, Melinda was totally polite and respectful. She even shook his hand and congratulated him on his victory.

It was the weirdest thing of all about Melinda. Just when you thought you had her figured out, she'd do the exact opposite of what you expected. Gates was bug-eyed. I think she scared him.

As for Shelby, I don't think I really was in love with her. That was probably just McMurphy.

* * *

Why did I let Melinda push me around? Sure, she was stubborn and determined, but she wasn't the Mafia. All I had to do was say no and stick to it. I never did.

For some reason I was incapable of standing up to the girl. I definitely wasn't attracted to her. She wasn't exactly my type, with the black clothes, black hair, black lipstick, black nail polish, and black tattoo. The only thing that wasn't black was the nose ring (gold). Not only did she adore punk bands with names like Purge and Sphincter 8, but she had to look like them too.

Don't get me wrong. On the weirdness scale at our high school, she was no more than a seven. But Melinda wasn't the girl next door, unless you lived at 1311 Mockingbird Lane, and your neighbors were the Munsters.

It's not that I didn't try to assert myself. I knew her every bit as well as she knew me. The punkier and more gothic she got, the less she fooled me. Punks are raw-meat people, not macrobiotic vegetarians.

But every time I was about to tell her off, I would remember that day back in fifth grade. Our fathers used to take the same train into the city every morning. It was Dad's turn to get the coffee. And by the time he returned with the two hot cups, Mr. Rapaport had collapsed on the platform. Heart attack. He never woke up.

My father quit his Wall Street job at the end of the same week. He bought a small hardware store in town.

So every time I was ready to unload on Melinda, I would back off and let her have her way. Guilt, probably, for having a father when she didn't.

[2]

HIGH SCHOOL REPUBLICANS: I KNOW what that sounds like—a bunch of preppy dorks who are too short for basketball and too skinny for football, so they track mock stock portfolios and talk about what model of Range Rover they're going to buy someday. But honestly, we weren't that bad. We didn't look down on everybody else. We were just doing our thing. And it didn't hurt that in the process, I was sticking it to McMurphy. I didn't know much about my genetic hitchhiker, but I was reasonably sure he wasn't a Republican.

So I hung out with Gates, and Fleming and Shelby, who were hot and heavy by then. Luckily, I was over her, but I suspected McMurphy was still carrying a torch, because nothing gave me more satisfaction than getting the better of Fleming. When my virtual stock portfolio beat his at the end of junior year, I was so overjoyed that you would have thought the fifty-six million dollars in it were real.

Melinda never gave up on trying to liberalize me.

"It's just a school club," I defended myself. "I haven't turned into a heroin addict."

She would have preferred me hooked on drugs. "Sixteen, and all you care about is how much money you'll be making a decade from now. P.S.— should I barf now or later in the privacy of my own home?"

"What's wrong with money?" I demanded. "We're going to have to get jobs at some point. Why not get a good one? If I have to work all day, at least I'll have something to show for it."

"Oh, almighty dollar, we pledge obeisance to thee!" Melinda had been in drama until the Big Dustup. (There are no goths in *Bye Bye Birdie*, and Melinda wouldn't wear Capri pants if you threatened her with an ax.) "What about fun? What about love?"

"Rich people fall in love." The fact that I was defending my life choices to someone who had once tried to wear the thin bone of a chicken wing through her nose was an irony that didn't escape me.

She didn't even hear. "What about ideas—

staying up until four in the morning dissecting a great book or a great film? What about art?"

"It's a fantastic investment," I told her. "Do you know what a Renoir goes for these days?"

I don't know why I worried so much about her sensibilities. She was the toughest person I knew. While we were in the middle of this conversation, some jock from the basketball team was trying to pass behind Melinda with his lunch tray. She had a way of straddling the cafeteria bench that placed her bulky black-and-chrome biker boots in everybody's way.

As the guy squeezed by, he muttered "Freak," under his breath. I'm surprised she heard it. I barely did.

Without missing a word of her righteous lecture about books, films, and art, she snapped up a black-clad elbow into the bottom of the guy's tray.

It was a marvel of physics. Not one drop of Salisbury steak and mashed potatoes missed him.

The jock wheeled on her. "Hey—!"

She froze him with a look. It wasn't a threat; it wasn't even a challenge. It announced, as clearly as if it had been spoken aloud: *Your opinion equals one tiny turtle turd.*

Aloud, she said, "Whoops—involuntary muscle spasm."

He decided that wearing his lunch from chest to crotch was a fair exchange for avoiding the unpleasant scene that was surely brewing. He quickly spotted some basketball buddies and hurried over.

Melinda turned back to me. "What about music?"

I knew that was coming. Melinda wasn't just a music fan. She lived and breathed music. At least she called it music. I wasn't exactly cutting edge, but I like to think I had some taste. The stuff Melinda picked to worship was the God-awfulest noise to come out of anyone's nightmare since the old A-bomb tests at Yucca Flats. Even the genre names sounded more like a gangster's rap sheet—punk, thrash, headbanger, metal, hardcore.

The fact that I didn't like it went without saying. But I couldn't even figure out what made it music.

"Look," I ventured. "You care about what you care about. Let me care about this. How many times have you lectured me about accepting people's differences? This is my difference. Accept it."

"I'd accept it—if it were the real you."

How can you argue with someone who knows everything?

Luckily, I had another friend who really *did* know everything. Good old Gates. It would be exaggerating to say that he'd memorized the Internet—but not by much. It was Gates who figured out that Melinda was actually KafkaDreams, a regular contributor on Graffiti-Wall.usa, the online billboard. Graffiti-Wall's motto was "Upload, Download, Unload," which sounded like Melinda's style, the unloading part, anyway. Still—

"How do you know it's her?"

He handed me his PDA, an old Casio he'd rewired to receive radio signals from Andromeda. "Take a look."

KafkaDreams Wall of Shame,

Worst of the Worst

Top (bottom) 5:

#1—War. Nuff said. P.S.—Camouflage sucks.

#2—Jocks. Just cause you can put a ball through a hoop doesn't mean you own the world. Wake up and smell the Desenex.

#3—Homophobia. I'm forming a hate group prejudiced against intolerant people.

#4—Young Republicans. What a bunch of bozos. P.S.—Haven't seen this much constipation since the great Ex-Lax embargo.

#5—Two words—Tater Tots. Two more— Obesity Epidemic. COUSCOUS RULES!!!

I turned to Gates. "How'd you find this?"

"I scanned the traffic that was routed through the school's server," he explained.

"All of it?"

"I did a search for 'couscous.' She talked about it on the boat trip—about how the buffet was a coronary waiting to happen."

He was right—Gates was always right. This was Melinda to a T. But why would a computer superstar with a billion things on his mind waste his time on it? Unless—

"You've got a crush on Melinda?"

He didn't deny it. "What's wrong with her?"

"She looks like a vampire," put in Fleming from the depths of *The Wall Street Journal*.

"Go back to your stocks," I told him. *I* could put Melinda down, but coming from Fleming, it got on my nerves.

Gates shrugged. "I think she'd clean up nice."

Fleming peered out from behind his newspaper. "Dude, you're going to rule the world someday. The president of Microsoft can't be married to a mutant."

I faced Gates. "You're serious—Melinda."

"Yeah." A goofy grin split his face. "She's—feisty."

"Melinda *Rapaport*?" I wasn't giving him a hard

time. I was struggling to see what he saw. I'd known her my whole life, but I'd never once conceptualized her as a *girl*. Especially not under all those layers of gothica. She was the last person you'd ever match with Gates, who was not just brilliant, but more than a little on the nerdy side. A guy like that should run a mile at the sight of her. Even her Web postings seemed more suited to an anarchist than a high school girl:

12-18

We go to school every day. Why? Because it's the law? If nobody showed up, what could they do? Put us ALL in jail? We're such sheep! P.S.—Baaah!

1-17

The problem with wimps is that they're too wimpy to know what wimps they are.

2-10

Life's too short to be nice to people you hate. While you're nodding and smiling at some jerk, the clock is ticking. Pretty soon you'll be dead, under a hunk of marble that says, "Here lies an idiot who wasted his life being polite to people who didn't deserve it."

Feisty? Crazy would be more like it. Gates ought to have his head examined!

My eyes fell on the latest entry:

> 3-22
>
> Seven years since Dad died. Can still see his face, but can't seem to call up his voice anymore.

Every time I think I've got her pegged, something happens to remind me that Melinda may as well be from outer space for all I understand her.

"I know somebody who likes you," I told her the next day at lunch.

She looked at me like I had shot her dog. "Don't mess with my head, Leo. You've seen what happens to people who mess with my head."

"Do you want to know who it is, or not?"

"Well, obviously you're determined to tell me," she said. "So go ahead."

And when I gave her the name, she didn't even know who Gates was. She remembered him as Caleb Drew—nobody's called him that since he first got his pudgy fingers on the keyboard of a laptop.

"That guy?" She was annoyed. "Quit pulling my chain."

"Honest—the guy likes you! I'm telling the truth!"

"But he's one of *you*," she argued. "The forces of steal-from-the-poor-and-give-to-the-rich. P.S. —he doesn't even know me."

I didn't want to admit that Gates was onto her secret Web identity. She'd think he was a stalker or something. "He admires you from afar. That happens, you know."

"I would never date a Republican," she said flatly.

"Well, if he asks you out, just say no—don't make a political speech," I pleaded. "He's a good guy, even if he has lousy taste in women."

"Hey, I'm flattered. I'm the only thing he's looked twice at that doesn't have a forty-gig hard drive."

Here's another example of the sheer audacity of the girl. In the middle of putting down *my* friend, she had the nerve to hit me up to tutor *her* friend Owen Stevenson in algebra.

"Forget it," I told her. "If Gates's feelings mean nothing to you, Owen's algebra grade means even less to me."

In an outraged instant, her black fingernail was

positioned half an inch from my left eye. "You're homophobic!"

"I don't have a problem with Owen being gay!" I defended myself. "I have a problem with him thinking he's smarter than everybody else!"

"He's gifted," she insisted. "And that doesn't just come from me. It comes from the state of Connecticut."

"Then why does he need a tutor?"

"Math is his weakness."

I snorted. "And English, history, geography, science—"

"Not true!"

"He isn't even good at being gay. When's the last time you saw him with a boyfriend?"

"When's the last time we saw *you* with a girl-friend?" she shot back. "I guess you're not very good at being straight."

I refrained from pointing out that if Melinda hadn't forced herself onto that boat trip, Shelby Rostov might very well be my girlfriend.

"You know how it is with Owen," she persisted. "They make him take all honors courses. He doesn't have a choice."

She was right about that. At the age of six, Owen had scored 180 on an IQ test, wowing his teachers and the Connecticut Department of

Education. They'd slapped a "genius" classification on the poor kid that he just couldn't shake. It never occurred to anybody that maybe the 180 was a fluke. Owen was a bright enough guy, but he was never going to live up to all those expectations. Yet whenever he tried to switch out of honors everything, the school wouldn't let him. Connecticut still believed in its diamond in the rough. The diamond had no voice in the matter.

"He got a raw deal," I conceded.

"You can help him," she wheedled. "You're great at math—McAllister Scholarship, early acceptance to Harvard—"

She talked me into it. I wasn't gullible—I knew she was snowing me. She just plain bulldozed it through. Senior year, up to my nose in exams, with Harvard on the line if I couldn't maintain my grades, I was donating my free periods to tutoring the untutorable.

Owen allowed me to work with him. That's just the kind of guy he was. Of course, I wasn't *helping* him; we were studying together.

"I hear you've been having trouble with vectors."

Owen looked me up and down. "That shirt isn't really a good style for you. You need a full collar to de-emphasize your Adam's apple."

If my Adam's apple was big, it bulged to twice

the size when I had to deal with Owen. "Let's just do this," I grunted.

"Okay," he agreed. "Explain to me the part you don't understand."

That's how the lessons went. *I* wasn't tutoring *him*. *He* was tutoring *me*.

Apparently, *I* had a mental block about vector kinematics. For three weeks, I explained it upside down and underwater. I might as well have been speaking Swahili.

Every day, Melinda asked me, "How's it going?"

And when I replied, "Not well," the look she shot me clearly said that she blamed my failure on homophobia.

We tutored on. I can't say I didn't learn anything: my voice was a little too high; my pants were pleated when they should have been flat front; I could never be a hand model with knuckles like that. What I *didn't* learn was vectors, which was to say *he* didn't learn vectors.

At last, a breakthrough. Owen loved old-fashioned pinball machines. So I used the path of a pinball as it bounces around the game to represent vectors. Each bounce has distance and direction, and the algebraic tally of the vectors is the final position of the ball.

Sound familiar? It was my pinball theory. Of course, I never applied it beyond the field of algebra until after I'd learned the truth about McMurphy.

And he got it. I knew he got it, because he said, "I think you'll be just fine now."

I bristled. "Hey, man, I knew this stuff already."

"See what we can accomplish when we work together?"

"You're delusional," I informed him.

But Melinda was pleased. And even though her opinion should have meant zero to me, I basked in it. I even checked Graffiti-Wall.usa to see if KafkaDreams mentioned my accomplishment. The closest thing I found was:

> Am toying with the possibility that people aren't
> such total boneheads after all. I think it might
> be PMS.

For security reasons, the senior algebra classes took the big test together in our cafeteria. That was how I wound up at the same exam table as Connecticut's former 180 IQ.

I shouldn't have cared. I'd done more than my bit for Melinda's friend. But when I saw Owen sitting there, lost at sea—*again*—I couldn't keep my eyes off his test booklet. Sure enough, he was on question twelve—vectors.

I wanted to scream. I thought of three weeks of study hall, countless hours, searching for a way to get through to that guy. And at last, success—or so I'd thought.

He forgot it! He actually forgot it!

So I took the fateful step. "Owen—" I hissed. "The pinballs! Remember the pinballs!"

I felt a hand on my shoulder.

[3]

LUCKILY, MR. BORMAN LIKED ME. ONE of the big advantages of the Young Republicans was that I had a decent reputation among our teachers. They thought I was going places, which reflected well upon the school.

But talking during an exam—that didn't look good.

"Copying answers from Owen Stevenson." He frowned at me over his reading glasses. "Why don't you explain what's going on here?"

I told the truth. "I didn't copy from Owen. I've been tutoring him during study hall. It wasn't cheating, Mr. Borman. He *knows* this stuff."

The assistant principal shuffled some papers and shot me a glance that was suspiciously like a smirk.

A little confused, I forged on. "He was having a hard time with vectors, but he finally got it. I didn't give him any answers. What I said was a buzzword to jog his memory a little."

He sat forward, eyes alert. "So what you're saying is, it was Owen who did the cheating, not you."

"No," I insisted. "Nobody cheated. It was just—"

"I think I know what cheating is," Mr. Borman interrupted. "You said yourself that Owen didn't understand vectors. He made you give him the answer. That's a violation of school rules."

"But that's not how it happened," I protested. "He didn't ask me for an answer. If anything—" I fell silent. The last thing I wanted to do was get myself in trouble over this.

"You'd better speak up, Leo," Mr. Borman warned me. "There was an ethics violation, and someone is to blame. You're a gifted young man with a bright future. If it wasn't you, now is the time to say so."

An alarm bell went off in my head. Mr. Borman had no interest in giving me a hard time over this non-incident. He was gunning for Owen.

I almost understood it. I mean, here was this kid who showed up with a file a foot thick from the Connecticut Department of Education proclaiming him to be this mental messiah. Paperwork up the wazoo as the state painstakingly nurtured its little jewel into adulthood. And it all would have been worth it if Owen really was a genius. But by high school, the IQ thing was ancient history, and he was no smarter than the rest of us.

"It's admirable to tutor another student and take a leadership role," Mr. Borman went on. "But you're a man now; your actions define your character—what you say, what you do, the company you keep."

And I just knew. There were plenty of reasons to find Owen annoying, and I subscribed to most of them. But that wasn't what Mr. Borman was getting at. He didn't like Owen because Owen was gay.

I felt *him* then—my genetic hitchhiker. It was *my* jaw stiffening, yet the cussedness making it happen was all McMurphy.

For a year and a half I had been a Young Republican, talking about things like character, when what was really on my mind was getting into Harvard and how Shelby Rostov probably looked in a bra and panties. But *this*, McMurphy seemed to be telling me, was the true meaning of character. Could I face myself in the mirror if I let the assistant principal use me to set up another student?

"I didn't cheat, Mr. Borman," I said gently but firmly. "And neither did Owen."

"Careful, Leo. Someone is going to pay for this. You should make sure it isn't you."

McMurphy and I stood up. "If that's all, I've got a class."

Whatever friendliness this meeting once had, it was gone now. Mr. Borman glowered at me. "Think about what this means, Caraway. Do you want a black mark like this on your permanent record?"

"I didn't do anything wrong," I repeated, and got out of there before McMurphy said something I'd regret.

All day long I suffered the tortures of the damned. For years, my genetic hitchhiker had been safe under lock and key somewhere inside me. What a time for him to show up again. When my permanent record was on the line and I had early acceptance to Harvard!

By the time I got home, I was a basket case. I locked myself in my room and called Mr. Hazeltine, my adviser from Harvard admissions.

I must have sounded pretty desperate, because he was kind to me. "Take it easy, kid. Harvard doesn't care about one test once you're already accepted. If you get a diploma, your place here is secure."

I allowed myself to breathe again.

"I heard you got caught cheating on the big algebra test."

Fleming placed his tray next to mine on the cafeteria table.

Shelby sat down beside him, her luminous eyes all concern. "What happened, Leo?"

"Big misunderstanding," I mumbled. "You know Borman. There's no talking to the guy. I won't bore you with the details."

"You weren't copying off that Stevenson kid, were you? Because that's what people are saying."

I snorted. "If I ever have to copy off that guy, save me a cyanide capsule. I took a zero, and it's all over."

"Well—" Fleming wasn't comfortable. "I don't want to be a jerk about this, but the club rules say your record has to be clean to be an officer."

The club was what Fleming called the Young Republicans. Like we had our own golf course or something.

I was disgusted. "Who came up with a stupid rule like that?"

He looked surprised. "You did."

"Don't worry," I promised. "I'll straighten it out."

"Hey, Leo." Melinda plopped her tray down across from me. "Hi, Shelby, Flem. How's the portfolio hanging?"

Fleming didn't like being called Flem, he didn't like Melinda, and he definitely didn't like discussing his portfolio—at least not until Pfizer bounced back.

Melinda swiveled on the bench and waved Owen over to make a fifth. That pretty much completed my joy.

Owen had an unerring capacity to say the absolute wrong thing. "How'd you guys do on the algebra test?" He had the gall to look inquiringly at me.

"You know exactly what I got," I growled, "and why I got it."

"Well, I'm done," Fleming announced, having wolfed down his entire sandwich in record time. He turned to Shelby, who had taken a grand total of three bites from her lunch. "Ready, Shel?"

"I'm still eating," she said, a little annoyed.

Fleming swept her tray out from under her and began dragging her away. "Keep me posted, Leo," he tossed over his shoulder. "The club needs to know."

"That guy is majorly constipated," Melinda observed mildly.

Owen nodded wisely. "He needs to get in touch with his gay side."

I choked on my V8. "Gay side? Fleming?"

"He suppresses it," Owen explained. "That's what makes him so—"

"Republican," Melinda supplied.

Desperate to change the subject, I picked up the sheaf of papers from the edge of Melinda's tray. "What's this?"

"My English project," she replied. "I've been working on it since Christmas."

"It looks like a PhD thesis," I commented, glancing at the title page: "Poets of Rage: A Sociological History of Punk and Its Offshoots." Twenty-seven pages. "I pity your teacher."

Owen stuck up for her. "What do you know about music?"

"More than you know about vectors," I returned bitterly.

And that would have been the end of it—if it hadn't been for that damn Web site.

Ever since Gates had alerted me to Melinda's blog on Graffiti-Wall, I'd been checking in periodically to see what KafkaDreams had to say. And even though I disagreed with most of it, I found it strangely compelling. It wasn't so much Melinda's commentary on life, the universe, and Tater Tots that captivated me. It was the fact that she had fans—real Web-surfers from all over the world who genuinely derived enjoyment and spiritual guidance from Melinda's oddball ideas. Like DarthLightning03 from Missoula, Montana, who wrote:

> rock on kd, u grok the BIG UNREALITY, boycott
> all government till somebody in washington
> gets a Mohawk, u'r the greatest, u totally suck.

Sucking, I gathered, was a *good* thing on Graffiti-Wall. It was used as high praise in many postings.

There was also CzechBouncer from Prague, who became emotional when Melinda mentioned living in the United States:

> My American jewel, you restore my faith in
> superpowers, be my oracle, be my guru, sorry
> can't worship you in person, your country may
> be strong, but the beer tastes like—

Some kind of content filter apparently kicked in here, since the sentence was never finished. It led me to suspect that CzechBouncer was actually writing from a computer in his middle school in Prague or possibly New Jersey. Just because the guy claimed to be European didn't mean it was true.

KafkaDreams made no direct response to her admirers. Instead, she wrote:

> Hey guys, forget the jocks, the senators, the principals, and all those morons who don't get it and never will. Smash your CD collections, melt your parents' vinyl, chuck your iPods. This is what it's all about!!!

Posted directly below that was Melinda's essay: "Poets of Rage: A Sociological History of Punk and Its Offshoots."

> This is the music of the damned, the anthems of outcasts and addicts and felons. From the scum of the earth comes the assault of distorted guitars, the shriek of vocals barely reclaimed from the depths of madness, boiling over in waves of anger and frustration. It is the roar of not just songs, but revolution, and the world will never be the same again.

Leave it to Melinda to take the crappiest music

ever recorded and turn it into an earthshaking historic event. But give her credit—I was reading it. How could you not? I was mostly interested to see what she could possibly say to back up those outrageous statements that her topic was anything more than garbage noise. Believe me, if I'd switched off my computer in disgust then and there, the course of my life would have been radically different, and I would have saved myself one cavity search in the bargain.

According to Melinda, punk had its roots in the 1960s. But the genre itself came into being in 1970s New York, and went prime time with the British band the Sex Pistols toward the end of the decade. In the '80s, punk dropped off the radar screen (maybe all its fans had gone deaf). The underground scene was alive and well, especially in L.A. But no punk group stepped forward to carry the Pistols' banner until 1984, with the arrival of Purge, the undisputed "angriest band in America."

Behind the tortured lyrics and vitriolic rants of front man King Maggot, Purge united the disparate tribes of hardcore and heavy metal, forging the headbanger's road map for years to come. For that reason, Melinda believed that the key moment in the modern history of punk was the formation of Purge by guitarist Neb Nezzer and King Maggot himself, born Marion X. McMurphy.

The room became a vacuum as I wheezed every molecule of air into palpitating lungs.

McMurphy.

[4]

A SILVER BALL RICOCHETING ACROSS the angled tabletop of a pinball machine, battered by flippers, jolted by bumpers, snared in traps, and just as suddenly sent careening around again. It was the image that taught Owen Stevenson vectors.

It was also the story of my life.

My first run-in with the flippers happened before I was born, but I wouldn't feel the sting for another ten years. Fourth grade—the field trip to Montreal.

You don't need a passport to travel to Canada, but you have to be able to prove your citizenship. Mom dragged my birth certificate out of mothballs, and she was plenty weird about it. Dad too, although he covered it up a little better.

Something didn't make sense. My name was on the document, but my last name wasn't Caraway. It was Davis, Mom's *maiden* name. Even stranger,

Dad wasn't on there at all. On the line marked "Father" was typed—

"Marion X. McMurphy?" I read. "Who's that?"

He had a look on his face like the gas company had started digging in the exact spot where he'd buried that dead body last year.

He cleared his throat carefully. "It's nothing for you to worry about."

"That's easy for you to say. What if Canada won't let me in? I'll be the only kid who doesn't get to go because there's a mistake on my birth certificate."

Mom: "It's not—*technically*—a mistake."

"Technically?" I turned to Dad. "You mean your name used to be Marion X. McMurphy? Did you get beat up a lot at school?"

I was sent out of the room so my folks could have a heated argument in whispers. I couldn't pick up every word, but Dad's refrain was, "Don't you think it's time we told him?"

"Tell me what?" I called through the doorway.

My father faced me. "Leo, I love you more than anything on this earth. I've loved you since you were a little baby—"

"No!" my mother barked. "Over my dead body—"

"He has the right to know," Dad insisted. "He'll have to know sooner or later."

"Then let it be later," she pleaded. "Much later. Like when I'm dead."

To this day, I believe the only reason they finally did tell me was because I looked so cowed that even the truth couldn't possibly be as awful as what was running around my terrified imagination.

Dad took a deep breath. "What I'm trying to say, son, is—I'm your father in every way but one. Biology. Your biological father was a man named McMurphy."

"What do you mean, biological father? What are you talking about?"

My mother tried. "You know how babies are made, Leo. When a man and a woman—"

"Oh, come on," I interrupted, "I know all about sex—" And then it hit me. "You mean you had sex with Marion X. McMurphy?" I wheeled on my father. "Dad! Why didn't you stop her?"

"I didn't know your mother when you were born," he replied stiffly. "Or when you were—" His voice trailed off. "Haven't you ever noticed that you're ten, and your mother and I just celebrated our ninth anniversary?"

I kept waiting for them to tell me it was all a joke—a sort of April Fools' Day in October. They never did. Eventually, Dad went to lie down with a splitting headache. But Mom had been steeling herself for this confrontation for a long time. She was prepared to go all fifteen rounds.

To her credit, she never once told me it was none of my business. It obviously very much was. But she refused to discuss word one about the man who had contributed fifty percent of my DNA. On that, she would not budge.

So I went on the class trip, and McMurphy went with me, on my birth certificate and in my veins. Canadian immigration officials didn't mind him. But I did.

I wasn't quite me anymore. Leo Caraway wanted to see St. Joseph's Shrine and Old Montreal. It was McMurphy who acted up and spoiled the trip for everybody else.

"Leo, what's gotten into you?" my teacher exclaimed.

She'd hit the nail right on the head. Something *had* gotten into me—or more precisely, some*one*. I'd try to be good. I'd try to be interested. And then I'd feel McMurphy rising.

I don't recall the specifics of my misbehavior, although it has become legend in the faculty room of my elementary school. At one point, I allegedly climbed over the railing of a freeway overpass and tap-danced on the concrete precipice while traffic zoomed by forty feet below. I was probably lucky not to have fallen to my death, which might explain why I've suppressed most of the details.

Mrs. Novak sent my folks a letter after the field trip was over. For weeks I waited for Mom to bring up the subject. She never did. She knew exactly what had ailed me in Canada.

"You've got to control yourself," Dad told me.

But he was wrong. I had to control McMurphy. I even called it that in my mind—The McMurphy Solution, or Project X. Of course, McMurphy shared that mind with me, which was kind of a security breach. That was the scariest part—were my strange impulses coming from my genetic hitchhiker, or were they my own, manufactured by paranoia, because I knew I wasn't alone in there? After all, I'd been a pretty normal kid *before* I'd learned about McMurphy, hadn't I? It became an obsessive game for me, replaying my entire life. Every misstep, broken rule, and temper tantrum—had that been *him*, hovering just below the radar screen?

By high school, Mom had filled in a grand total of zero details regarding my birth father. But as I got older, I became savvy enough to bombard her with some alternate theories of the crime:

"What was it, Mom? Soft music? Candlelight? Rohypnol in your ginger ale? Contraceptive failure? Beaker mix-up at the sperm bank?"

My mother would have made a great secret agent. Even under torture, she would reveal absolutely nothing. If I pressed the issue, she'd pull a jigsaw puzzle out of a cabinet, and begin fitting pieces together. To watch her painstakingly assemble a reproduction of the ceiling of the Sistine Chapel, just to avoid telling me the story of my own origin, was maddening beyond belief.

She'd murmur generalities while searching for the right corner piece. "I was very young then, Leo." Or "I wasn't thinking straight."

I couldn't let it lie. "Were you drunk? High? Feverish? Did you get bitten by a tsetse fly?"

"There are no tsetse flies in Connecticut," she informed me. "It was more like temporary insanity. Now, I don't want to talk about it anymore. It's in the past for both of us."

"Was he a quarterback?" I persisted.

And when she took out a 1,500-piece macro-puzzle of an extreme close-up of the inside of a pomegranate, I howled, "That's why I need to know! *I* wouldn't ask such a rude question! That had to come from the McMurphy side of me! Don't you get it? I'm carrying around a time bomb, and I don't know when it's going to go off!"

At least now I had the answer to that question—April of senior year, while reading "Poets of Rage" over the Internet.

[5]

I CHECKED THE NAME AGAIN. SOME-
times your eyes play tricks on you.

Marion X. McMurphy.

If it had been just Marion McMurphy, I could
have told myself it was a coincidence. But how
many Marion X. McMurphys could there be?

One. My biological father. It was a bull's-eye, a
lightning strike.

I'd always assumed I'd learn about my father in
the long run. But it would be from Mom, and only
when she had covered every tabletop and flat surface in our house with acres of jigsaw puzzles.
Whoever thought that such pivotal, life-altering
information would come from Melinda Rapaport's
essay on punk rock?

For God's sake, the guy was *famous*! A legend,
practically, if you went by Melinda. I scrolled
through the pages. And what a legend! Convic-
tions for destruction of property, drug possession,

public indecency, civil disobedience, resisting arrest—everything but murder!

Melinda listed these crimes like they were his accomplishments, not his rap sheet. In the Old West, people like this were strung up from the nearest tree; in the '80s they became rock stars.

I'd always blamed my McMurphy DNA for every weird urge and character flaw, but that was just neurotic. Never did I seriously believe that I'd turn out to be so spectacularly *right*! I mean, a dad in the entertainment industry would have been kind of cool, but *this* was more like terrorism than show business. The blood of a notorious lowlife flowed through my veins.

I was Prince Maggot.

I went through every word of that essay, devouring the details about this rock star who had fathered me. Even in the rebellious antisocial world of punk, King Maggot was considered a bad boy. Those warning labels they put on CDs—all that started because of Purge!

Purge's idea of a cute publicity stunt was to call a press conference and then hold the reporters hostage for two days. Everyone thought it was staged, but the band did three months in jail for that. All the proceeds of their next album went into paying the fines and reimbursing the city of New York for the use of their SWAT team.

Once, when Purge suspected their lawyer might be skimming money from the band, King Maggot drove a three-thousand cc Harley through the plate glass window of the man's office, and threatened him with a samurai sword.

Dear Old Dad was more than a rock star. He was the cultural boogeyman of his time. When Purge came to town, parents double-locked their doors; church groups picketed the performance venues; even the Teamsters called in sick to avoid having to unload equipment for the hated band. The president himself called Purge un-American, which made sense except, on the other side of the Atlantic, they were considered un-British too. Norway turned them back at the border on their 1986 world tour. When their song "Bomb Mars Now" hit number one on the charts, *Billboard* magazine refused to print their name, leaving the first line of its famous Top 100 blank.

Purge broke up in 1990, when the angriest band in America had become too successful to be all that angry anymore. They were gone, but not forgotten. Scores of punks, rockers, ska bands, even some hip-hop artists, listed Purge as their biggest influence. That included Melinda's current favorite group, the Stem Cells, a band so abundantly talented that she described them as "the next Sphincter 8." High praise. "But," she wrote, "there will never be another Purge."

When I finished the essay, I wasn't done yet. Google came up with 175,000 hits on the key-words "King Maggot." I thought of the years I'd spent *agonizing* over the identity of my stealth sire. If I'd bothered to do a simple Internet search, I'd have learned the truth on day one.

But who could have believed the guy would turn out to be an icon? My mother was Sally Average, puzzle fanatic, book-group member, Oprah fan. For her, cutting-edge music was Pink Floyd. Her only addiction was to frozen yogurt. Even when she worked, she still managed to be a stay-at-home mom—like when she got her real estate license and couldn't sell a single property. (She just enjoyed seeing the inside of other people's houses.)

Her and the punk Elvis?

I binged on information about Marion X. McMurphy, so long a mystery, and suddenly so vividly real. It was like witnessing a car accident—the details were awful, and yet I couldn't bring myself to look away.

Born in Wichita on July 23rd, 1961, Marion

Xavier McMurphy attended Kansas State University, where he was a business major with hopes of becoming a CPA.

If that one sentence was divorced from everything else ever written about this man, I could almost have understood how he might be a relative of mine. This was a person who fathers a Young Republican.

Then I scrolled down to his picture, circa 1985, age twenty-four. It wasn't technically a Mohawk, but the head was shaved on the sides, and multicolored spikes marched up the crown. He had two black eyes—not the color. I mean shiners. Around his neck was a hangman's noose over a ripped white T-shirt, which featured a happy face with an ax buried mid-skull. He wore one earring—a dangling electric chair. The hand that held the microphone sported brass knuckles.

But his face—that was something else. The eyes bulged; the veins stood out. He seemed to be on the verge of biting the head off the mike and spitting it out at the audience. I had never seen such pure unadulterated rage. If Purge was the angriest band in America, this was its angriest member on one of his very angriest days.

I looked for a sign—the barest hint—of family resemblance. Nothing. If I could have taken a special pill to put me into a homicidal fury, then maybe I would have had a basis of comparison. This looked more like a vicious dog than a human being.

I was so thoroughly transfixed by the image on the screen that I never noticed my parents had wandered upstairs. My mother walked straight into my room and spotted the picture on my computer screen.

It might have been the start of a very long conversation if she hadn't gasped and fainted dead away.

[6]

"YOU USED TO BE A *GROUPIE*?"

A vast underwater panorama of the Great Barrier Reef covered our kitchen table. Mom was hunting up and placing pieces with the concentration and driven intensity of a chess master. The puzzle was a megalith, with enough eye-poppingly microscopic fragments to assemble the reef one coral polyp at a time. She went for it the instant she came to, leading me to believe she'd bought it years ago, with exactly this day in mind.

"Not a groupie," my nonbiological father said sharply. "You're talking about your *mother*, Leo."

"Well, how else would she meet that—that guy?" I demanded. "Or was I conceived through the mail?"

Mom glanced up from a school of yellowtail long enough to say, "We're not discussing it."

My McMurphy impulse—King Maggot impulse, I guess—was to sweep the entire puzzle onto the floor. Then she'd have no choice but to confront this head on. I tried a different tack. I took a tiny piece, part of the lower jaw of a grouper, and set it in place.

That small act—working *with* her instead of against her—seemed to draw her attention from the puzzle. She seemed almost dazed, as if waking from a deep sleep.

Gently, I said, "You have to discuss it. It's *my* story. This is how I came to be."

Dad backed me up. "Donna, the kid's seventeen. He's going to Harvard in the fall. It wasn't Immaculate Conception. He has the right to know."

And there, leaning over a scene out of Jacques Cousteau, she told me. She looked like she was facing a firing squad, but I give her credit. She came clean.

"I thought we were going to the movies," she mumbled, eyes averted. "But Cynthia, my friend, surprised me with tickets to see Purge at some club in New Haven."

I was amazed. "You *like* that kind of music?"

"Well, not really. But it was right after King pulled that stunt with the Harley. Everybody was talking about Purge. Anyway, we were at the show, and one of the roadies invited us to a backstage party. And we met the band." She looked at me, her eyes imploring me to understand. "I worked as a bank teller. My life was so boring. This man was a rock star, and he wanted to hang out with *me*."

I was amazed. "So you were, like, King Maggot's girlfriend?"

She grimaced. "It was just that once. I had a lot to drink and there were—drugs. To tell you the truth, I don't even remember that much about it."

I opened my mouth to say something, but she cut me off. "Can't you see what an awful memory this is for me, Leo? I could never regret having *you*—that's been the best thing in my life. But the way it happened—how can I talk about it without setting a bad example for you?"

So now I knew. After seven years of total, almost pathological preoccupation, the great enigma was over. And it didn't solve anything or make me feel any better.

That night was the first and last time I posted a comment on Melinda's blog. KafkaDreams had set up a message board for people to give their opinions of "Poets of Rage." Mine was this:

It changed my life.

She'd never know how much.

Of course, I didn't realize it then, but I was another big step closer to Detective Sergeant Ogrodnick and the cavity search.

I'd been in music stores before. But when I stepped into the HMV at the Brickfield Mall, I felt everyone looking at me, as if I were naked or something. And when I found the rack devoted to Purge's discography, I half-expected somebody to say, "Checking out the Old Man's albums?"

But nobody could know who "the Old Man" was.

Still, going to the register carrying a CD entitled *Sewer-cide* made my cheeks hurt.

The cashier was impressed. "Oh, I love that one! The first time I heard it I shaved my head."

A ringing endorsement.

I listened to it on a Discman, of course. The last thing Mom needed was to hear her old mistake screaming the house down. The next voice screaming the house down would have been hers.

There weren't a lot of punk Republicans, and *Sewer-cide* offered nothing to add me to the list. The guitars were muddy, loud, and relentlessly pounding. All I could get from the drums was that someone was beating them to a pulp. The vocal was a violent harangue—against what I'm not entirely sure. It was impossible to make out what King Maggot was bellowing. It was just too distorted, a cross between ranting and quacking.

The CD cover listed all the songs in order: "Bomb Mars Now," "Number Two," "The Supreme Court Makes Me Barf," "Bleed Me" . . .

I couldn't connect the titles with the vocals, or even tell where one track stopped and the next began. Okay, I wasn't exactly a fan, but should it be so hard to understand what you're listening to?

I tried. Honestly I did. I set aside all my opinions about punk and approached it as an intellectual exercise. Nothing. No melody. No rhythm. I might just as well have headed to the nearest airport and listened to them revving up jet engines.

I stuck *Sewer-cide* so far in the back of my sock drawer that it was practically not in the room. Nothing was different. Finding out was just a hiccup; Project X was still on. Now that I knew I was harboring a McMurphy far worse than my wildest nightmares, it was more vital than ever to keep the guy under control.

I woke up at three o'clock in the morning. The CD was trying to interface with my McMurphy DNA. I could feel it out there, like a fax signal waiting for another fax to make a connection.

Tomorrow, I resolved, I would bury it in the

backyard. If that didn't do the trick, I was prepared to carry it to Mordor and hurl it into the fires of Mount Doom.

The next day at lunch, I admitted something to Melinda that ordinarily I wouldn't have confessed under torture.

"I was listening to *Sewer-cide* last night—"

"Don't patronize me, Leo," she interrupted with a snort.

"Hey," I defended myself, "I listen to music."

"Oh, yeah. Kenny Chesney and Zamfir, master of the pan flute."

I bristled. "You're the one who's always calling me a musical Philistine. Forgive me for taking the initiative and trying something new."

Owen was humming tunelessly and drumming on the cafeteria table with a plastic fork. I was so amazed to find that I recognized the un-melody that I actually sang a few words along with him: "Bomb Mars, now; nuke Mars now . . ."

Melinda was round-eyed. "I can't believe you got turned on to Purge! So? How much did you love it?"

I shrugged. "I didn't shave my head, if that's what you mean."

"No, seriously. It's the greatest punk album of

all time. Lacks some of the oomph of *Apocalypse Yesterfunk*, but more sophisticated musically."

"Well—" I probed further, "what do they mean by bomb Mars? Even if we could get bombs to Mars, what would be the point? There's nobody there."

"Don't you get it? We're always bombing somebody. Why not Mars? Nobody makes a statement like King!"

Being one of those statements, I couldn't really argue with her. But the songs still made no sense to me.

"What about 'Number Two'? What's the message there?"

"That's my favorite," Owen enthused. "We spend twelve years in school, but to the system, we're nothing but a bunch of test scores—Number Two pencil marks for computers to read." That made sense for a guy who'd spent most of his life trying to outrun his own IQ test.

Melinda nodded. "Things like that get King nuts."

"Seems to me just about everything gets King nuts," I observed sourly.

"That's why Purge is so great," she explained. "We think it and feel it, and there's King screaming it over a hundred thousand watts of raw power.

It's like your words are pouring out of his mouth, and his rage is your rage. It blows your mind!"

Look, it was still just noise, and I couldn't make out a note of it. But the mere fact of knowing it was about something—*anything*—gave me some small comfort. It made King Maggot a little less of a wild beast.

McMurphy, that poltergeist in my veins, was a real person. In all the years that I'd been sharing a body with the guy, that thought had never once crossed my mind.

[7]

MAY. THE HOMESTRETCH. HIGH SCHOOL, for all intents and purposes, was over. The big exams had all been taken. Grades—at least the ones that would be reported to colleges and universities—were already set. Class attendance was sparse, and even the teachers didn't seem to mind.

The buzz was about next year—who would be going where. Melinda had final acceptance from U. Conn., and four schools were actually competing for Owen. Despite average SATs and lukewarm grades, Connecticut's diamond in the rough would be cruising to a full ride somewhere. At least it meant Borman wouldn't get his way.

Gates was (where else?) Stanford-bound, and Fleming and Shelby both got the nod from Yale. Somebody had to be the sickening lovebirds of the incoming freshman class, I guess. I was just happy they'd be sickening somebody else for a change.

At our next Young Republicans meeting, good old Flem brought in stacks of newspaper clippings claiming that his Yale had surpassed my Harvard in the college rankings. What was the point in arguing? High school arguments seemed lighter than air, and getting lighter.

Harvard was stamped all over my incoming mail—dorm assignments, preregistration. Some fraternity even sent out a flyer advertising their first party of the fall. The tuition bill was there too, along with a letter from the McAllister Foundation. They were the sponsors of my scholarship, the only way I was able to pay said tuition bill. So it was fitting that the two should arrive together.

I tore open the McAllister envelope. The letter was short and to the point:

Dear Mr. Caraway,

We are sorry to inform you that we are canceling your scholarship funding due to a recent ethics violation we note in your student record. In addition to academic and extracurricular achievement, the foundation requires the utmost in integrity from our candidates. In this light, we cannot overlook what your school describes as "cheating on an examination."

With regret,
Rosalie McAllister Black
CHAIRPERSON

It was like being hit by a train when you didn't even know you were standing on railroad tracks. Total devastation, but total shock as well. I had checked with Harvard after my meeting with Borman. In a million years it had never occurred to me that the math test thing would cost me my scholarship. If it wasn't a deal-breaker for Harvard, why should the McAllister people care?

A feeling of cold panic descended on me as I realized that a no on the scholarship was a no on Harvard, too. Sure, I had college savings, but that would never cover more than a state school. Dad owned a small-town hardware store; Mom picked up a few extra bucks as the dispatcher for substitute teachers in our area. My first year's tab for tuition and housing was more than *forty thousand dollars!* For me to come up with that kind of money now would take a much larger ethics violation than the one I'd allegedly committed with Owen Stevenson. I would have to hold up an armored car on its way to Fort Knox!

I was screwed.

My parents took it worse than I did.

"If only we'd *known*, Leo!" Dad lamented. "We could have found that money somewhere!"

"Come on, Dad. Forty grand? That was always the deal—no scholarship, no Harvard. That's why I applied to state schools—in case the McAllister didn't pan out."

"But we told the state schools to forget it!" Mom interjected desperately. "It's too late for that now!"

Dad cut right to the heart of the matter. "But how can they accuse you of cheating? *Did* you cheat?"

"Of course not!" I exploded. "I was tutoring a guy in algebra, and I said one word to him in the exam. One word! It wasn't a question or an answer."

"But why did you say *any* word?" my mother persisted.

"Mr. Borman was gunning for Owen Stevenson," I explained. "If I'd served the kid up on a silver platter, nothing would have happened to me."

"Owen Stevenson?" my mother repeated shrilly. "You can't stand Owen Stevenson!"

"Borman's worse. He was looking for an excuse to kick Owen out of school, and I sure wasn't going to do his dirty work for him."

They supported me. Mom got on the phone to Mr. Borman, and Dad took on the McAllister Foundation. Then they switched. They fought hard for me, their strident, outraged voices ringing through the house.

In the end, it was all settled. The powers that be were going to take away my scholarship, and I was going to let them. There's no mercy in academia.

Screwed.

Thinking back on it, I probably should have gone to the newspapers to expose Borman for the tin-plated dictator that he was. But that wouldn't have gotten me my scholarship back. Technically, I was in the wrong here. Talking during an exam counts as cheating. It's like speeding—everybody does it, but if you're the guy they catch, you're done.

Dad was practically suicidal. "This is my fault. If I had stayed on Wall Street that tuition bill would be a drop in the bucket right now."

"Erik, that's crazy talk," my mother soothed.

"Who could blame you after what happened to Dan Rapaport?"

"There were a lot of other guys on that commuter platform, and none of them quit their jobs. None of them put themselves ahead of their families."

"You did that *for* your family, remember?" she argued. "So you'd always be there for us."

It tore me up to see him blaming himself for this. I also saw a connection with that day on the railway platform, but my take was different. Ever since then, I'd been unable to say no to Melinda. If I'd had the spleen to tell her to stuff it when she'd asked me to tutor Owen, none of this would be happening right now.

If only life came with a rewind/erase button.

"Oh, Leo!" Mom was distraught. "I know defending Owen was the right thing to do. But, oh honey, how *could* you?"

It came back to me as clear as Caribbean water—the feeling that had swelled inside me as I'd sat opposite Mr. Borman, stiffening my jaw as well as my resolve. Only this time, McMurphy had a face—ferocious eyes blazing beneath a punk haircut.

I bit my lip. This was probably not a good time to bring up King Maggot again.

* * *

I moved through the halls of that school like I'd never seen the place before. I could barely walk in a straight line. I wasn't drunk. It was just that my life had suddenly become entirely devoid of direction. I felt like a guy who had just been released from prison after serving a fifty-year term. This was not my planet.

The planet may have been different, but the local aliens were still the usual suspects.

"Leo! *Leo!*" Melinda came pounding down the hall, her layers of black on black flowing behind her like the cape of the vampire Lestat. "You're never going to believe this! It's the greatest thing that ever could have happened!"

I made a split-second decision then and there: I would tell no one that I wasn't going to Harvard. I couldn't face the questions and I couldn't face the sympathy. People might get suspicious in September when they saw me still working my summer gig at Dad's hardware store, but they weren't going to hear the news from me.

"What's up?"

"Guess who's headlining the Concussed World Tour this summer?"

"The *what*?"

She was disgusted. "Concussed, Leo. They

have it every year. It's a traveling all-day festival of punk, hardcore, ska, and heavy metal. You're going to die when you hear the news: Purge is getting back together to do the tour—all the original band members!"

It should have made a big impression on me—the fact that my biological father was about to slither out from whatever rock he'd been hiding under since 1990. I'd never really thought of him as a today person. He was just a guy who, eighteen years ago, made some terrible music and got my mother pregnant. The fact that all his fame was from the '80s only seemed to reinforce the idea that he existed in the *past*.

Now he was going to resurface.

Before yesterday, that would have been front-page news. But now, with my life in shards around my feet, I had no interest whatsoever in seeing the mysterious King Maggot in action. If Purge had been staging their reunion in our backyard, I wouldn't have lifted the blind to check it out. Losing Harvard had done that much for me. McMurphy couldn't hold me for ransom anymore. There was nothing left for me to lose.

Anyway, your real father wasn't the one who provided the genetic material. He was the one who was willing to get on the phone and call

Rosalie McAllister Black an "unreasonable, heartless old bag." Dad was a real pit bull; Mom too. And even though it hadn't changed anything, it was some consolation to have two people so ardently on my side.

I felt a surge of resentment toward Melinda for interrupting the end of the world to supply me with this useless information. That might have explained why I snapped at her the way I did.

"What makes you think I care?"

She looked at me as if I'd slapped her.

"I've got news for you, Melinda. Purge sucks! All punk sucks! It's stupid, pointless noise!" It was the first time I'd raised my voice since opening the McAllister letter. It felt good to let the anger out, even if it was being directed at the wrong person. "Look at you—you've based your whole life on it! What does that say about *you*?"

I'd seen her deck goth-hating jocks in a single blow, with the silver studs of her dog-collar bracelet pulled up onto her knuckles. But when she punched me, it was barely a tap on the shoulder with the soft leather part. It hurt far worse than a home run swing, because I knew how much my words must have upset her. She expected to take grief from the usual gang of loudmouths at our school. But not from me.

On the other hand, if I'd had the guts to offend her a couple of months ago, I might still be going to Harvard.

So why did I feel even worse than before?

That Saturday, Owen Stevenson dropped by to see me just before seven A.M. His 180 IQ may have been a thing of the past, but he was still gifted in the field of bothering people.

I blinked bleary eyes at him, struggling to find focus. "Don't you sleep?"

"I just got off the train from New York," he replied. "Mel and I stayed up all night waiting in line for passes to the Concussed kickoff press conference."

"Congratulations." I mumbled. "That's the dumbest thing I've heard all day. Of course, it's early yet. Plenty of time for you to say something even dumber."

In spite of the fact that I was blocking the doorway, he pushed past me and established himself in a living room chair. "Mel was going to get a ticket for you too, as a surprise. You know—*before*."

"I'm glad she didn't bother. I wouldn't be caught dead in that place."

Another funny thing about Owen. If you don't tell him what he expects to hear, he continues as if you hadn't spoken. "You were really nasty to her. What did she do to deserve that?"

"For starters, she saddled me with you." I gave him my most inhospitable glare. "Now, are you here just to bug me, or do you have something to say?"

"You don't know how good a friend Mel is to you," Owen informed me. "When people make fun of you and your Young Republicans, she doesn't let them get away with it. When people are sick of hearing about your Harvard scholarship, she sticks up for you. When people call you a snob—"

"What people?" I growled. "It's you, isn't it?"

"It's lots of people," he insisted. "And you should hear Mel—'Leo's a good guy; I've known him my whole life; he's just a little misguided.' What do you say to that?"

"Since when is 'misguided' a compliment?"

"You owe her an apology."

Here's the thing: I'd been mentally formulating an apology to Melinda for the past two days. But I wasn't going to admit it to Owen.

I said, "Go home."

He stood up. "I told her not to get you a ticket, but she got you one anyway. You're going to see Purge."

"I've got better things to do with my time than to waste it on a bunch of middle-aged punks who were *nobody* in their prime, and are even less now."

He faced me with haughty dignity. "Twenty-five million CDs—what do you say to that?"

"I don't know," I told him. "What the hell are you talking about?"

"Twenty-five million CDs and vinyl records—that's what those *nobodies* sold in their prime."

"Really?" I stared at him, stunned. A lapsed Einstein, sure. But he had just pointed out something I'd never thought of before.

Rock stars weren't just notorious bad boys and gossip column fodder. The music business *paid*! Twenty-five million CDs—that was a lot of money. And that didn't even include concerts, T-shirts, posters, and radio and TV royalties!

Here I was, completely undone by losing a forty-thousand-dollar scholarship, when . . .

I had a rich father!

[8]

I SAT ON THE PACKED TRAIN, WEDGED in between Melinda and Owen, on my way to the press conference and an uncertain future.

Good old Melinda had forgiven me readily. God only knew why. Just like I couldn't stay mad at her, she apparently couldn't stay mad at me. Maybe it was our shared history, which stretched clear back to toddlerhood. Maybe she wasn't as punk as she liked everybody to believe. Or maybe she was just so psyched about the prospect of a Purge reunion that everything was sunshine and roses. On her usual online soapbox, KafkaDreams posted this message:

> Nobody bug me today. This is the greatest
> moment in the history of recorded time! Tell you
> all about it tomorrow, but right now I'M GOING
> TO SEE PURGE!!!!

Her enthusiasm hadn't dampened on the train. "I can't believe," she was raving, "that when we get there, the four guys sitting behind the microphones are going to be Purge. I mean, what do they look like now? Has anybody seen them in all these years? King used to be so sexy!"

Owen nodded thoughtfully. "But you know who's smokin'? That guy who calls himself Ylang Ylang—the drummer for the Ball Peens."

Melinda shook her head. "The real hottie is Pete Vukovich from the Stem Cells. P.S.—he has the best butt in punk."

While they giggled like sixth-graders, I sat there, working up a migraine, scared witless. I felt a lot like those Olympic athletes who train for decades, and then it all comes down to a ten-second race. How was I going to get close enough to King Maggot to give him the letter I'd written, explaining who I was, and how I desperately needed to talk to him? Would he read it? And even if he did, how seriously would he take it? Rock stars collected paternity claims like baseball cards. I could be one of a royal court of thirty Prince Maggots.

I had thought that getting into Harvard and competing for a McAllister scholarship was pressure. I didn't know the meaning of the word.

On the subway ride down to the SoHo Grand Hotel, those two got talkier, and I sank even deeper into my personal sensory deprivation tank, until I felt like a disembodied brain, floating in formaldehyde.

Melinda noticed my anxiety. "Leo, are you okay? There's no color in your lips." Her voice seemed to be coming from a long distance away.

Owen beamed triumphantly. "I knew you were going to have a great time!" Like being pale and ill was a barrel of laughs.

When I saw the hotel ballroom, my heart sank through the soles of my shoes. There must have been eight hundred people in that room, packed bumper-to-bumper. The close-in section was roped off for the press. We squeezed into the back of the peanut gallery with a bizarre mix of neo-punks and middle-aged housewives—black leather and body piercings pressed up against L.L.Bean and minivan keys.

I was a light-year from the dais. To get King Maggot's attention from this distance, I'd have to spontaneously combust. How was I going to get closer?

I shouldn't have worried. Melinda had no intention of being this far from the bands. As the interviews started, she took our hands and began to ooze us forward through the crush of people until we were right up to the velvet rope that separated the spectators from the press.

There were nine bands signed on for the Concussed tour—the Stem Cells, Dick Nixon, the Ball Peens, Mark Hatch and the Hatchlings, Skatology, Chemical Ali, Lethal Injection, Citizen Rot, and the immortal Purge.

Since they were the headliner, Purge was scheduled to go on last. That meant we had to endure three hours of the other groups, a collection of unkempt, nose-picking thugs who didn't have a word to say that was more than four letters in length. Each was determined to shock by being more rude/outrageous/nasty/obscene/stoned than the others, the net effect being that they all sort of blended together into a mass of generic cave dwellers.

The crowd had their favorites here and there. Melinda snapped dozens of pictures of the Stem Cells, and Owen went pretty wild when the Ball Peens took their place on the dais. Dick Nixon's drummer had just gotten out of jail, so he was the object of a lot of media interest. But it was pretty obvious that everybody was waiting for the main event. Like me, they wanted to see the return of the legend.

We all had to sit tight. After three interminable hours, they declared an intermission, and everyone was served a free eight-ounce bottle of water, and presented with a plastic bagful of premium giveaways—a T-shirt, baseball cap, bumper sticker, pencil, and refrigerator magnet, all embossed with the Concussed logo, in which the O had been turned into a round head that was being bashed in by a sledgehammer. The tongue was hanging out, and the eyes were X's. A spray of blood splattered the other letters.

By the time the MC returned to his microphone, we'd all been there for close to four hours. At that point, people would have gone crazy if they'd introduced the four Teletubbies. So when Purge took the stage, there was bedlam.

The biggest noise came from the forty-somethings we'd left in the back of the room. They were shrieking, howling, and even spitting, which Melinda explained was a sign of deep respect in the '80s punk scene. Now I understood why they'd given out baseball caps. I put mine on, and so did everybody else.

After the parade of strutting freaks we had just witnessed in the form of the other eight bands, the sight of Purge—the freakiest of the freaky—was a little surprising. They could have been the freaks' fathers, or at least their cool uncles. They were a generation older, and not quite so willing to do absolutely anything just to get attention. They were still punks—at least they were trying to be for the tour. But it was obvious they were coming off a long stretch as civilians.

Max Plank, the drummer, sported a Mohawk that faded into his receding hairline. Zach Ratzenburger, bass, now hid a big paunch beneath his bullet-perforated leather jacket. Neb Nezzer, the guitarist, incorporated a strange limp into his macho strut, and was obviously favoring a bad back.

And then my eyes fell on the fourth member of the group—the lead singer and front man; the father of modern punk, not to mention me. I had sweated out the last four hours, and a ninety-minute train ride before that, my head lost in a whirlwind of figuring the angles of a desperate scheme to salvage the future. Yet the moment I laid eyes on King Maggot, a strange calm came over me.

This was McMurphy. The McMurphy on my birth certificate, the McMurphy in my veins. Somehow, the fact that I was standing there, looking at the missing piece in the puzzle of who I was, eclipsed Harvard, tuition money, and all my machinations. This was my father, my blood.

Although, family resemblancewise, I could see zilch.

Melinda was in ecstasy. "Look at them! They haven't changed a bit!"

Obviously, the eyes of love were blind, and fame was a glow that smoothed over wrinkles and colored gray hairs.

Of the four, King Maggot was the best preserved, mostly because he was slim and still had a full head of dark hair. But something was missing in his case as well. I startled myself by actually knowing enough about Purge to realize what it was. The white-hot rage wasn't there. The leader of the angriest band in America looked like he only wanted to kill two or three people instead of the usual five hundred.

The ovation lasted ten long minutes. And it wasn't just us. The press people applauded. The other bands came back out to cheer. You'd think Purge had cured cancer, and not recorded "The Supreme Court Makes Me Barf."

When order was finally restored, Max Plank stepped forward to speak for the band. "Nobody panic. We're not taking hostages this time."

It got screams of appreciation, and the questions began.

"King, what have you been doing for the past sixteen years?"

His reply was the first words I ever heard from the mouth of my biological sire: "Ask your mother."

I felt like he'd just spit in my face. If it had been *eighteen* years, they could have asked *my* mother.

"Zach, what's the best part of being back together again?"

"Stupid questions from people like you."

"Neb, how did you keep your guitar skills up during the years off?"

"Picking zits."

All the answers were like that, and nobody seemed to mind or think it was unusual. This interview had nothing to do with information. It was to give the band members a chance to be obnoxious in public, almost as if the fact that they could fire off a nasty comeback proved that they really were Purge.

"King, have you still got your motorcycle and your samurai sword?"

"Give me your address and I'll get back to you."

In fact, in the entire press conference, there was only one question that got a halfway straight answer. It was this: "Hey, King, the other guys all have families. What's your story?"

King Maggot raised his mirrored sunglasses, revealing dark piercing eyes that were, for the moment, devoid of anger, genuine or manufactured. "Nothing to tell," he replied. "I just never had any kids."

And that statement jolted me out of my stupor and galvanized me into action.

"No!" I said aloud. "That's not right!"

Melinda looked at me warningly. "Leo—"

I ducked under the rope and pushed my way into the crowd of media.

"Beat it, kid!" a newsman told me. "This is press only."

But I was not going to be stopped. This event was already running an hour late. Someone was going to shut it down any minute, and then my chance to reach King Maggot would disappear forever.

I reached back and yanked the camera out of Melinda's hand. I put the viewer to my eye and bulled forward, snapping pictures of the back of a lot of reporters' heads.

"Hey, quit pushing!"

When at last the sea of obstructions opened up, and the viewfinder showed a clear path to the band, I hurdled the front barrier and ran for the dais, shouting, *"King! That's not true! You do have a kid! I'm your son!"*

I got within ten feet of Purge before two large

roadies sandwiched me, effectively stopping my progress. I bounced off, reeling, and pulled the letter from my back pocket. I held it out toward King, but he made no move to take it.

A very large hand closed on my shoulder and spun me around. Frantically, I yanked myself free and Frisbee-ed the envelope in the direction of the band. I saw it bounce off the chest of a startled Max Plank before the roadies—four of them now—each grabbed a limb and carried me to the exit.

"Read the letter!" I howled. *"There's proof!"*

They toted me down a fluorescent-lit corridor in the guts of the hotel. I became aware of a sudden cool breeze, and then I was airborne, still hugging Melinda's camera. A moment later, I found myself in a place most Young Republicans don't frequent—lying across a pile of green garbage bags in a deserted alley. As indignities go, it didn't measure up to the cavity search that lay in my future, but it was a respectable, if distant, second.

I leaped up and started banging on the metal door. But it was locked from the inside. No one answered.

I prowled the alley, looking for another way in. The doors were all bolted shut. Most of them didn't even have outside handles. I took stock.

Garbage in the alley meant that sanitation people could get in. So I could get out.

It wasn't a short trip. The outlet was on the other side of the block. I had to race around two corners before I could even see the marquee of the SoHo Grand. Then I couldn't get near the front door because of a huge milling crowd.

"Hey!" A kid about my age was pointing at me. "There's the guy who tried to attack King!"

It hit me—these were the people from the ballroom. The press conference was over!

I looked around. The nucleus of this seething mass was a silver stretch limo parked at the curb. All I saw of the band was a phalanx of roadies and the receding Mohawk of Max Plank as he ducked his head getting into the car.

I knew this would be my last chance. *"King! It's true! Read the letter!"*

The car door slammed shut, and the limo began to inch away.

A man twenty years older than me sneered in my face. "Hey, King—I'm the kid's brother! You're *my* father too!"

"You're my mother!" piped up another comedian. "You're my step-cousin twice removed!"

The smoked glass receded, and I caught a glimpse into the limo. King sat surrounded by his bandmates, looking in my direction. But behind those mirrored glasses, it was impossible to tell what his eyes were fixed on. If anything.

I took one more stab at it. *"Mr. McMurphy—"*

But at that moment, the stretch broke out of the crowd and disappeared down the SoHo street.

I hope I never again experience the despair I felt standing there, watching it go.

I hung around the dispersing throng, looking for Melinda and Owen, but they were nowhere to be found. After half an hour, I gave up and hopped on the subway to Grand Central.

Maybe it was for the best. I wasn't in the mood to have to talk to Melinda about what I said to King Maggot, and mostly, why I said it.

I made the train by the skin of my teeth, and passed between cars, looking for an empty seat. Sure enough, there were my travel companions. I took the bench across from them, and handed over Melinda's camera.

She snatched it from me. "Go away."

"Let me explain—"

"I don't want to hear your explanation," she snarled. "If you hate my music, you could have just said so. You didn't have to bust up Purge's first press conference in sixteen years."

I stared at her. "Is that what you think happened today?"

"Music is important to me, Leo! Every bit as important as being an Ivy Leaguer is to you!"

"Didn't you hear what I said in there?" I cried angrily.

"The whole world heard what you said," she snapped back. "Really smart. Stuff like that may be a big hoot with you Republicans, but in the rock and roll business, paternity is not something you joke about."

"I wasn't joking! That guy is my father!"

"Oh, sure," she said sarcastically. "Then who's the bald man with the white Taurus who sleeps at your house?"

"That's my dad. But he's not my biological dad. He met my mother when I was a baby. They *told* me!"

"They're lying," she said, tight-lipped.

"Why would they lie about something like this? It doesn't exactly make my mother look good. The letter—the envelope I tried to give King. It had a copy of my birth certificate. And the name under father is Marion X. McMurphy!"

In answer, she got up and stomped away to sit in another car. I waited for Owen, her shadow, to scamper off after her. He just sat there grinning at me.

"Thanks for the support," I told him.

He shrugged. "*I* believe you."

This was the last thing I expected, and from the last person. "Yeah? How come?"

"Because you look just like him."

I stared at him dumbly.

After a moment, he said, "Mel believes you too, you know."

"She's got a nice way of showing it."

"You know what?" he offered cheerfully. "I think she's going to come around."

This from a person who thought Fleming Norwood of the Westport Norwoods had a gay side. I wasn't holding my breath.

Anyway, the real mess today had nothing to do with any self-styled goth-punk. It was about me, and how I'd tried to reach out to my biological father.

And failed.

The future of my friendship with KafkaDreams was irrelevant. I had no future, period.

It rang a bitterly ironic bell. According to "Poets of Rage," "No Future" had been the original title of the Sex Pistols' classic "God Save the Queen." Melinda called it the second most powerful punk refrain of all time, after "Bomb Mars Now."

I felt its power then, that was for sure.

When I finally straggled up the driveway, physically and emotionally drained, Dad was waiting for me at the door.

"Listen, Leo, before you come in, there's something you should know. You made the six o'clock news."

"Oh, God! Did Mom watch it?"

Behind him, I could already see the answer. From our living room carpet rose the upended stern of the sinking *Titanic*. It was the biggest puzzle my mother owned, a 3-D tour de force of 6,000 pieces, too large to fit on any table in the house.

"How bad was it?" I asked. "What did they show?"

"Not much," he assured me. "Just a few seconds on how Purge still has what it takes to get people riled up. Then you came busting through the crowd and made a run at the band."

My heart sank, "Could you hear what I was saying?"

"There was no audio. But your mom reads lips. Anyway, we didn't figure you were at that press conference for the fine music and genteel company. So? Did you meet him?"

I shook my head. "A bunch of roadies picked me up and threw me in the garbage. I guess they cut to the weather before that part." I studied my sneakers. "Dad, I made a total idiot out of myself."

He put a sympathetic hand on my shoulder. "Let me buy you a drink." We went into the kitchen, and he poured a couple of Cokes. "I understand why you went. In your place, I probably would have done the same thing. He's your father, after all."

"*You're* my father," I retorted. I hadn't planned on making a confession, but once it began, the floodgates opened, and the words came tumbling out. "I didn't go to New York looking for my roots. I went looking for forty thousand dollars."

Dad stared in shock. "Leo!"

"He can afford it! Mom never asked him for any child support over the years. This is the *least* he can do!"

He had no further comment. But I had only to glance at him to put the finishing touches on this perfect day. It was plain to see by his sorrowful expression that I had disappointed the only father who mattered.

"Don't look at me like that," I mumbled.

"I won't stop you," he told me sadly, "because there's no way I can lay my hands on that kind of money. I talked to a mortgage broker, and he said the most we could squeeze out of the house was another twenty. We can come up with the rest, but not in time for September. Maybe not even by *next* September." He took a deep breath. "It doesn't exactly feel great for me, either. To know that I can't provide for my son, so he has to go chasing after a total stranger—"

"Dad!" I was horrified. "Nobody blames you! How many people could pull forty grand out of a hat?"

He made no reply, but the answer, though unspoken, hovered in the air between us: Wall Street guys could. This Harvard thing had Dad questioning his decision to quit his high-stress job and buy the hardware store. And rock stars—they had piles of money.

I realized that the shadow of Marion X. McMurphy hung over Dad's life just as much as my own. Maybe even more so, considering the circumstances. To have me suddenly pursuing my biological father *now*, sixteen years after Purge had left the spotlight, had to hurt. I'd just poured salt in that wound.

"Well, you've got nothing to worry about." It was all the comfort I could offer. "They wouldn't even let me talk to him."

But that wasn't the point, and we both knew it.

[9]

THE DEFINITION OF "GET A LIFE":
Fleming Norwood phoning me six days before the
end of school to officially blackball me from
the Young Republicans.

"Hasn't a Yale man got more important things
to worry about?" I asked irritably.

Gates had already given me a heads-up that this
was coming, so I wasn't exactly shocked. He'd
even volunteered to quit in sympathy with me, but
what for?

Fleming didn't answer my question. "It's this
cheating thing. You said you'd straighten it out,
and—well, you never did."

"You've got me there, pal," I said with false
cheeriness. "I guess I'll have to suffer through
these last few days as an enlisted man."

"And you can't put the club on your resume,"
he told me. "Or use it in later life."

I had to laugh. "There is no high school in later

life, Fleming. Once we step out that door on Friday, the whole four years never happened."

I acted like I didn't care, but the truth was it bothered me. Not that Fleming had ever been my role model. But next year he'd be an Ivy League freshman with a beautiful girlfriend and infinite prospects, and I'd be—

God, what *would* I be? Depressed, maybe. Humiliated, probably.

A total loser, definitely.

Mercifully, the call-waiting beeped in. "Sorry, Flem—gotta take this." I hit *flash*. "Hello?"

"Leo Caraway, please," came a voice. English accent. All business.

"My name is Nigel Ratcliff. I'm an attorney." He paused. "I represent King Maggot."

King *did* get my letter!

"You must understand—my client is flabbergasted. It's an outrageous claim."

"Outrageous but true," I said.

"That remains to be seen," he informed me. "But let us assume for the sake of argument that you are my client's progeny. What are your intentions?"

"Intentions?"

"What, precisely, do you want from Mr. Maggot?"

Mr. Maggot. I stifled a laugh. Then it occurred to me what the lawyer was getting at: was I a gold digger?

The answer was—well, yes. I absolutely intended to hit King Maggot up for money. Not the way Ratcliff had in mind—I wasn't going to sue for millions or demand to be put in King's will. I just wanted the tuition for next year. Hell, it could even be a *loan*; between Dad and me, we'd pay it back somehow. I just didn't want to give up my spot at Harvard.

But if I mentioned money, Ratcliff would assume the worst. Then the opportunity would be gone forever.

"I just want to meet him," I lied. "I'm not a blackmailer or a stalker. I'm a kid who's looking for a chance to get to know his father."

There was pause. Then, "Are you free tomorrow afternoon?"

"Uh—I guess. But—"

"The St. Moritz Hotel. Room 1101. Shall we say two o'clock?"

We must have said two o'clock, because on that note, he hung up on me.

I put down the handset, mind whirling. What I'd been meaning to tell Ratcliff was I had school tomorrow. On the other hand, what could they do to me for ditching—put a black mark on my record? Kick me out of the Young Republicans?

School would get along without me.

I had a meeting with King Maggot's lawyer.

The St. Moritz Hotel, New York City.

The elevator stopped and I exited to the plush hall. A brass plaque declared Room 1101 to be the Presidential Suite. I stepped through the open door and found not a hotel room but a business office. A miniature mansion of connected luxury parlors had been converted into Concussed festival headquarters. At least a dozen publicists chattered excitedly into cell phones. Band members were being interviewed all around the suite. The breathtaking view of Central Park was obstructed by a hanging map of the United States, with festival venues marked with pushpins. A manicurist applied black polish to the fingernails of one of the members of Citizen Rot, while a stylist dabbed at his Mohawk with blue dye.

A roadie was stringing an electric bass with barbed wire, next to a woman who had passed out in the middle of the floor. People stepped over and around her. Others used her as a bulletin board. Her bare back and leather mini were covered in multicolored Post-it notes.

I stood in the doorway, waiting to be noticed, when a roadie appeared, bellowed, "Fan mail!" and upended a large canvas sack. An assortment of letters fluttered down, followed by a dead octopus that hit the floor with a splat. A note attached to one of the tentacles bore greetings from the staff at Lockjaw Records. Apparently, this was the punk equivalent of a bouquet of flowers and a good-luck card.

After ten minutes of being ignored, I approached a publicist. "I'm looking for Nigel Ratcliff."

"Anybody seen Nigel?" she barked.

"He left," supplied a middle-aged man standing in the hall.

I was devastated. "But I'm supposed to meet him here. At two o'clock."

"Sorry, kid." The publicist hurried away, but the man's wary eyes were still on me.

"Mr. Ratcliff wanted to talk about my letter," I forged on. "You know, the *letter*—" I wasn't sure how much I should say out loud.

He pushed his way over. "So you're *that* kid." He put an arm around my shoulders and led me into the suite. "I didn't recognize you without a half-ton of gristle clamped on."

"You were at the press conference?" I asked, a little sheepishly.

He nodded. "I'm Purge's manager. Bernie McMurphy."

I snapped to attention. "McMurphy—"

"King and I are cousins," he supplied, ushering me from the main parlor into a narrow hallway with rooms on either side. "So my interest is personal *and* professional."

I regarded him. There was no resemblance to King that I could see. Then again, King was clinging to his '80s punk look, and Bernie could have been the one-hour-photo guy at a small-town Wal-Mart. Except for the eyes. You don't know bloodshot until you've seen those eyes. Like he was in the middle of a lost weekend that had been going on for several months.

He nodded me into the next doorway. Inside, two people occupied a large leather couch. One was a young reporter, jotting shorthand notes on a ring-bound pad. The other was King Maggot.

Feeling like an intruder, I took a step backward, and inadvertently crunched Bernie's toe.

Spying me, King stood up. "Got enough?" he asked the reporter. It was a statement of fact rather than a question.

The young man took the hint and followed Bernie out. That left me alone with the biological father who was a complete mystery to me. Talk about confronting your demons. I was face-to-face with McMurphy.

He examined me so intently that it raised the hair on the back of my neck. This wasn't the usual homicidal stare of his stage persona. This was scrutiny. I was being scanned.

I have no idea where I got the nerve—probably from him—but I stared right back. If somebody didn't say something very soon, I was either going to laugh or cry. I wasn't sure which.

At last, he broke the silence. "Tell me about your mother."

Not "Hello"; "Good to meet you"; "So you're Leo." I mean, I wasn't expecting him to rhapsodize over what a fine young man someone had raised to be his son, but I'd hoped for a few syllables of pleasantry before we got straight to business. His speaking voice was low and surprisingly mellow.

"Her name is Donna—Donna Davis, back then. It was at a show in New Haven where you guys—met."

From my pocket I pulled a laminated photo of Mom bringing me home from the hospital and held it out to him. He studied it, but made no move to take it.

At long last, the verdict came down: "I don't remember her."

I could feel my face turning red. "That's it?"

He shrugged. "Nothing personal."

"It's personal to *me*!" I practically yelled at him. "It's the reason I'm alive! But you don't remember, so too bad, kid, take a hike."

He was surprised. "I'm not sending you away. I'm just telling the truth. I don't remember. I wish I did."

I wasn't sure exactly how to take that. After all, we were talking about my *mother*! Technically, I shouldn't want this old letch to remember *anything* about his brief encounter with her. On the other hand, it was plain that the act that began my life was completely meaningless and forgettable to this rock star. It really burned me up.

So he was a celebrity. So what? He wasn't even famous for the *right* reasons. It wasn't like he'd developed a vaccine or negotiated world peace. He was a cultural bad boy, worthy of attention only because of his outrageous behavior and his unflagging capacity to offend. Except for hearing-impaired counterculture nut-jobs like Melinda, everybody agreed there was zero value to his so-called music.

At that moment, I didn't care about Harvard or my future or even the fact that I was on his turf, and I would probably end up in the garbage again.

I was going to introduce my bio-dad to a little piece of himself. It was time for McMurphy to crash this party.

Just as I opened my mouth to let him have it, Bernie, the manager, poked his head back into the room. "So?" he questioned. "Are we related?"

"Definitely," said King without hesitation.

If he'd hit me with a brick, I couldn't have been more astounded. *Definitely?* What did he see in me that made him so positive? Was it my almost display of temper that would have knocked out the back wall of the hotel? As the real McMurphy, was he so attuned to rage that he could recognize it even in its potential?

"He has the ear," King told his cousin.

"The *what*?"

He took my hand and raised it to my right ear. "Feel that little notch in the lobe? It runs in the family."

He turned his head to the side so I could see the anomaly on him. Bernie picked up a small makeup mirror and held it out to me. I found the right angle and took in the sight of King Maggot's earlobe hanging off my head.

I looked at both of Bernie's ears. No notches.

He shrugged. "Not all of us have it. It skips the occasional kid. But if you do, you're a McMurphy."

So it was definite. Not that I'd ever doubted it, because why would Mom make up such a horrendous thing? But to be here, standing right beside the guy, seeing what a jumped-up, uncaring jerk he was, and *that's* when it gets confirmed—it was the living end. I felt like jumping out the window, but unless I was holding on to King at the time, what would be the point?

"We'll do DNA testing too," he told me. "To sew it up nice and neat for the lawyers."

I nodded. Of course he didn't trust me, or a romantic partner he didn't remember, or even the evidence of his own family trait. Only indisputable scientific evidence was enough for the great King Maggot. Every minute I spent with him, I liked him a little less. And he hadn't been very high in my estimation at the start.

"The final results take four to six weeks," he went on. "I think we should use that time to get to know each other."

My cheeks burned from the sheer hypocrisy of that statement. Purge was about to embark on a coast-to-coast tour. Concussed was scheduled to go to Europe in the fall. Get to know each other? How were we supposed to do that—by carrier pigeon?

Calm down, I told myself. Meeting King had been a lousy experience—offensive, dehumanizing, and generally unpleasant. Yet the most important part of all this had gone exactly right: the front man of Purge had pretty much admitted that I was his son.

I may have been out of the Young Republicans, but that didn't mean I couldn't be pragmatic and businesslike. There was a purpose to this whole exercise, and it wasn't for me to share a warm and fuzzy moment with the composer of "Bomb Mars Now."

In four to six weeks, the DNA people would confirm that I was one-hundred-percent Prince Maggot. Then and only then would I hit King up for my Harvard tuition money. Coming from his scientifically certified flesh and blood, how could he say no?

Getting to know this person—it was a small price to pay.

"I'd like that," I said carefully. "Maybe when the tour is over, we could—uh—have dinner or something."

He shook his head. "It's already been seventeen years. We can't waste any more time."

"Yeah, but you'll be on the road with the band. You're not going to be in—" I frowned at him. "I don't even know where you live."

"I live in Malibu," he told me, "but I'm not

talking about the occasional dinner. Why don't you spend the summer traveling with me?"

I was floored. "You mean—"

"With Purge," he finished. "On the Concussed tour."

It was straight out of left field, something I hadn't expected in a million years. This total stranger, who didn't even seem to like me, and must have sensed how I felt about him, was prepared to bring me along on his comeback tour—a thirty-city traveling punk rock festival that would make front-page news in every city it touched.

How could I say no? Forget that it wasn't my kind of music—and shouldn't have been *anybody's* kind of music. I wanted a future in the business world; *this* was big business, the blockbuster entertainment event of the summer. And I'd be a part of it, and see it from the inside.

King must have interpreted my silence as reluctance, because he sweetened the deal. "Don't worry about money. I'll take care of your expenses. And you'll have a job." He turned to Bernie. "Have we got something for Leo to do?"

He knows my name, I thought. It was the first time he'd spoken it aloud.

"I can always use another pair of hands," said Bernie. "Junior roadie. You'll like the guys."

"I've already met them," I replied, rubbing my bruised hip.

King grasped my hand and shook it, and actually smiled at me. In all the CD covers and publicity shots and Internet sites, I'd never seen him smile before. It didn't fit the image of the Angriest Band in America.

"Thanks for coming down," he told me. "I'm really looking forward to this."

Then he turned away, and I wasn't there anymore.

It took me a moment to come to terms with the fact that, in King's eyes, I had suddenly ceased to exist. It was Bernie who ushered me back into the main part of the suite, where the Post-it girl had awakened, and various Concussed officials were reclaiming their notes from her body.

The manager gave me a sympathetic smile. "You get used to King's style. When you're the *man*, you're like a drug, and everybody wants a toot. He's not shutting you out. It's just his way of making sure there's enough of him to go around."

I didn't reply. I was wondering if that's how it was with my mother eighteen years ago.

[10]

BERNIE WAS RIGHT ABOUT KING BEING like a drug. I must have been on *something*. How else could I have agreed to join a traveling punk rock festival without even considering what my parents were going to say?

The thought didn't occur to me until I was at a pay phone in Grand Central station, calling my dad to let him know what train I'd be on.

"Brickfield Hardware."

"Hi, Dad. I made the four-oh-eight. Can you pick me up around five-thirty?"

"No problem."

"One more thing"—sucking air—"I'm not going to be able to work with you at the store this summer. I—I've got another job lined up."

"Always the wheeler-dealer, huh, Leo?" he chuckled. "Okay, lay it on me. What's so important that it's worth leaving your old man shorthanded? You're the new president of the Stock Exchange, I suppose."

"I'm going to be a roadie for Purge."

There was a pause on the other end of the line. "Be serious."

"It's the truth." I filled him in on the details of my meeting with Bernie and King.

"Do you have any idea what goes on with a tour like that?"

"Do you?" I countered.

"When Purge comes to town, it's like a state of emergency! Cities hire extra police, impose curfews—"

"That was the eighties, Dad. They're all like *you* now—regular middle-aged guys. Besides, most of that stuff was probably hype. The media distorts everything."

"Can you be sure of that?"

"Look, it's all for Harvard, okay? If I had my scholarship, none of this would be necessary."

"And King Maggot agreed to fork over forty grand?" he persisted. "Just like that?"

"I haven't mentioned it yet," I confessed. "Not until the DNA tests come back. By then I'll have known the guy for a month, and I won't seem like a gold digger."

I could hear his unspoken response over the dead air: *Seem?*

"It's the only way, Dad. Trust me."

He was silent for another moment. Then: "I want to meet him."

"There's no time," I argued. "Concussed starts in a few days."

"If King Maggot wants to take *my* son on a thirty-city tour, first he's going to look me in the eye and promise me you'll be okay."

"Yeah, but you'll never get an appointment. He's got wall-to-wall interviews."

He came to a decision. "I'll be there in an hour."

I was horrified. "Dad—no!"

"The St. Moritz, right?"

Click.

Now I was nervous. I noticed something in Dad's voice that I hadn't heard in years. Not since the day he'd decided to give up the commuting life after Mr. Rapaport's heart attack. When Erik Caraway set himself on a course of action, you couldn't change his mind with a howitzer. He'd never drive a Harley through a plate glass window, but in his own way, he was just as hell-bent.

I called back, and got a recording. Dad was already on his way.

The meeting of my two fathers, regular and biological, was something I would gladly have put off until doomsday. Talk about a clash of opposites. King was a rock star; Dad owned a small-town store. King could pull forty grand out of petty cash; Dad was a regular Joe with regular finances. King had seduced my mother before Dad had even held her hand. Worst of all, it was King's DNA, not Dad's, that made up half the sole heir to Brickfield Hardware. Dad knew all that, and had accepted it a long time ago. But to stand next to Marion X. McMurphy—that had to be a bitter pill the size of a U-boat.

At five o'clock I stood outside the St. Moritz. It was another half hour before Dad emerged from the hotel garage, looking stressed and disgusted.

"Forty bucks for parking," he muttered. "If I can find a spot on the street the next thousand times I come to the city, I'll save enough money to pay your tuition."

"You don't have to do this," I urged gently.

"The hell I don't."

We went upstairs to the suite, which was, if anything, even more chaotic than before. The Stem Cells had arrived, and were prancing and mugging for a gaggle of photographers. Guitarist Pete Vukovich was shirtless, showing off a brand new diamond stud in his pierced nipple. I thought Dad was going to throw up.

"Come on," I chided. "To each his own."

But the piercing wasn't what offended Dad's sensibilities. "Poser," he scoffed. "When did you ever see Johnny Rotten with a two-carat rock in his boob?"

I pulled up short. "You know about this kind of music?"

"In high school we used to take the train into the city to go to CBGB. Everybody was there—the Ramones, Patti Smith, Television, the Dead Boys—"

"Purge?"

"They came later," he told me. "I'm talking about the early days, when punk was just starting out."

Could it be that Dad was more comfortable in this scene than I was?

Everybody was ignoring us. Worse, we seemed to be in the way. Photographers kept backing into us. Dad knocked over a TV crew's lighting rig, which nearly brained one of the Hatchlings.

Finally, he marched up to a small desk and barked, "Is King Maggot available?"

A young man with a reverse Mohawk—bushy hair on the sides and a bald stripe shaved down the middle—surveyed him up and down. "And you are?"

"His son's father."

Reverse Mohawk never even questioned it.

"King's in with *Rolling Stone* right now," he told us. "You'll have to chill."

We chilled on the edge of a leather ottoman, sharing space with a stray amplifier. As regular business hours drew on into evening, new people continued to arrive, rougher around the edges, if such a thing was possible. A room service cart packed with champagne bottles was wheeled into the suite. Someone cranked up the music—all I could make out was the refrain, which sounded like "kill the poor."

"Dead Kennedys," Dad supplied. "Early eighties."

The business office was transforming into a party. Women, dressed to shock, were trawling for rock stars. Pete Vukovich was the catch of the day. "Shove over, yo," he mumbled to us, joined at the lips to his hoochie. As they squeezed in beside us, she climbed onto his lap for space conservation and possibly other reasons.

"Let's get out of here," I hissed at Dad.

His expression would not have been out of place on the stone heads of Easter Island.

A hot buffet showed up on another room service cart, along with more champagne. I checked my watch. It was coming up on eight o'clock! Where was King?

And then a familiar earlobe appeared out of the throng, attached to the body of my bio-dad. Bernie was with him, steering the punk icon through the maelstrom of worshipful high fives that swirled around them. The cousins McMurphy looked tired and anxious to leave. But Bernie stopped when he spotted me on the edge of the ottoman.

"Hey, Cuz—have you been here all this time?"

It had to be the most awkward moment in history. "King, Bernie"—my voice sounded unnaturally high—"this is my father. I mean—"

Dad spoke up. "I need to talk to you, Maggot or McMurphy, or whatever your name is. You've only been a father for a few hours; I've been at it for seventeen years, so let me give you a little friendly advice: if you're going to let your kid go gallivanting across the country with a man like you, you'd better make sure he's not going to be exposed to anything sick." He tossed a thumb in the direction of Pete and his girl, who were approaching the "get-a-room" stage.

I waited for King to sic the goon squad on us. But the rock star didn't call for his army of road-ies. He didn't even seem to be offended. He looked like he was thinking it over.

Finally, he said. "What do you suggest?"

Dad, who had been anticipating a punch in the nose—and maybe even hoping for it so he'd have an excuse to pound King Maggot—was caught off guard. "Huh?"

"For Leo," King elaborated. "What special arrangements should we make for him?"

This left Dad hemming and hawing. That Purge's notorious front man might ask for a laundry list of demands was the last thing he'd prepared for. "Well, uh, he's not a baby. But he's not—you know—one of you."

"Fair enough." King stuck out his hand, and Dad shook it—an image still scorched on my retinas.

With that, King and Bernie were out the door and gone. Dad was shell-shocked. Maybe he was going over the conversation in his mind, searching for the place where he'd missed his chance to make a big stink. At any moment, he might burst out with, "And furthermore . . . !" only to find himself talking to the back of somebody's head.

But he just said, "What the *hell* are we going to tell your mother?"

[11]

OUR HOUSE LOOKED LIKE AN ART GALLERY tilted ninety degrees. Every table, counter, cabinet top, and a good percentage of floor space hosted an elaborate jigsaw puzzle. Images ranging from the Last Supper, to an aerial photograph of Mount Everest, to a scientifically labeled close-up of a tarantula festooned our home. The simple act of moving from room to room became a tightrope walk. Heaven help the poor slob who accidentally stepped on a completed work.

Mom was quiet in her focus, but that peacefulness was deceiving. When my toe accidentally dislodged one of the spiral arms of the Milky Way galaxy, Mom threw a book at me, which only served to knock a piece off Michelangelo's *David* that I'm sure David would dearly love to have back.

She scrambled to restore the famous sculpture. "Watch it, will you? I'm trying to do a puzzle!"

"You're not doing *a* puzzle," I retorted. "You're doing fifty puzzles because you won't face the fact that I'm going on Concussed."

Dad stuck up for me. "Don't treat this like it isn't real, Donna. Leo will be eighteen soon. We can't hold him back forever."

"I hope you told that degenerate we're holding him responsible for anything that happens on that traveling freak show!" she seethed at Dad.

"No worries," Dad assured her. "I set Maggot straight."

I didn't hear anything more from King, but Bernie faxed me directions to a nearby lab where he had scheduled my DNA test. A courier arrived with a packet of information about Concussed— festival venues, hotels, and maps.

I was with the band.

> tor•ture, *n*: 1) The infliction of severe physical
> pain as a means of punishment or coercion.
> 2) Having to march up on the graduation stage
> and shake Mr. Borman's hand (*see Caraway,
> Leo*).

"Leo's hard work over the past four years has brought him numerous honors, including early acceptance to Harvard," the assistant principal announced to polite applause as I accepted my diploma.

It made my blood boil. I mean, Borman knew exactly what had happened to my scholarship, and that, as things stood, Harvard was a pipe dream for me. And he had the *nerve* to take credit for my academic success while at the same time rubbing it in that I wouldn't get to go.

I was angry, but McMurphy wanted him dead. Just because I was going on tour with Purge didn't mean my genetic hitchhiker was under control. Now that he was not just my father, but also my employer, Project X was more important than ever.

I bottled up McMurphy and marched off the stage into the high-fiving mass of seniors. That was where I found myself nose to nose ring with Melinda. We hadn't spoken since the Concussed press conference.

"Congratulations, Leo," she mumbled.

"You, too. And you," I added to Owen, who had materialized over her shoulder. During the ceremony, Mr. Borman had gone on and on about Owen's gifted status in a fatherly *I-taught-him-everything-he-knows* tone. As if Borman hadn't ruined my life in his attempt to ruin Owen's. Was our A.P. a class act or what?

Melinda wouldn't look me in the eye. "So

did you ever get in touch with him?"

I didn't have to ask who she was talking about. "I met him. He's pretty nice."

This prompted a little gasp from her. "And?"

"We think it's probably true. Him being my father. I have the McMurphy ear." I flipped up my notched lobe. "We're doing DNA, just to be sure."

I waited for her to demand every detail of my conversation with the burning bush. Instead, she turned away. Funny—my history with Melinda was pre-preschool. We'd started with precious little in common, and seemed to have less every year. But even as she grew into a goth, and I grew into a Republican, we always got along. Who knew that the one thing that would come between us would be the one thing we actually shared?

King Maggot was her idol. You'd think that me being his flesh and blood would be good in her eyes. But she seemed to resent it, like I'd snuck up and stolen him from her.

The only normal comment came from, of all people, Owen. "That's really cool, Leo, finding your roots like that." Then he spoiled it by adding, "Your mom must have been totally hot before she got middle-aged."

"You have a nice summer too," I managed.

I couldn't get out of there fast enough.

[12]

WHEN ST. GEORGE SET OUT TO FIGHT the dragon, knowing he had an excellent chance of coming home a charcoal briquette, his mother probably created less of a scene than mine did at Kennedy Airport. She would have happily shipped me off to a dozen fire-breathing beasts rather than one King Maggot. In her eyes, I was going off to join the Klingons. I would come back grunting and scratching myself—if I came back at all.

She held it together all the way to security. Then, just as my laptop was heading through the X-ray, she blurted, "I'm sorry, Leo!"

I froze, my front leg partway through the metal detector. "For what?"

"I'm sorry I planted a stranger inside you, who you feel you have to get to know in order to know yourself!" she raved. "I'm not a bad person! I made one mistake a long time ago, and how can I regret it if that's what brought me you?" After years of stony silence and three-word answers, after enough jigsaw puzzles to fill Toys "R" Us, my mother was finally ready to share her feelings about how I had come into the world.

Oh, how I wished for a jigsaw puzzle of my own right then. It was all I could do to stammer, "Please don't worry about me, Mom," as I stepped through to the other side.

Even Dad looked a little rocky as the TSA agent was measuring my toenail clippers. "You can still change your mind, Leo. You don't have to do this just because you said you would."

"I'm fine," I promised. There was more I wanted to say, about how he was always going to be my one and only dad, no matter what happened. But we were holding up the line, and the clippers passed inspection. It was time to go.

It would be the last I saw of my parents before the cavity search. If I'd known then what I know now, I'd have been babbling just as compulsively as my mother.

The omens were bad from the outset. My tray table wouldn't come down. They ran out of Coke so I had to have diet. And somewhere over the Grand Canyon, an indicator light came on, signifying either catastrophic engine failure or a faulty indicator light.

We landed in Las Vegas, and sat there for about three hours. That's how long it took them to decide that, whatever the problem was, they couldn't fix it.

There were no more planes available, so they stuck us on a bus. Five and a half mortal hours later, we pulled into LAX. If anybody had come to meet me, they sure weren't there now. The L.A. show had already started.

Concussed was an all-day outdoor festival that kicked off around noon and went on until midnight or later. As the headliner, Purge didn't appear until last, so the band wouldn't even head over to the venue until later in the evening. But the roadies had to be there early, getting the equipment in place for when Lethal Injection was done, and it was time to set up for the main event.

It was already after nine. I was late for my first day of work. I unloaded my baggage from the bus's cargo bay and somehow managed to cram it all into a taxi. According to Bernie's faxes, the venue was an old, out-of-use racetrack in the San Fernando Valley.

The taxi driver was ecstatic. I found out why. It was a one-hundred-and-fifteen-dollar fare. I wanted to argue with the guy, but even outside the gates, the roar of raw punk was so loud that he wouldn't have heard a word I said. I paid up.

The cab drove away, leaving me grunting under two big suitcases and a backpack. The place would have qualified as the middle of nowhere, except for the presence of forty thousand head-banging fans, whipped up to fever pitch. The stage looked like it was in the next county. But the noise was up close and personal—two giant walls of speakers, blasting enough decibelage to move the San Andreas fault.

My eyes fell on a huge guy wearing an EVENT STAFF jacket. He wasn't a punk. He looked more like a Hells Angel. I pushed my way over and showed him my CREW badge. He glanced at it and waved me forward in the general direction of the eighty acres of surging, screaming humanity.

A hand clamped on to my shoulder. *"Leo!"* I only heard the voice because it was bellowing in my ear. A semi-familiar face—Cam Somebody. One of Purge's roadies, part of the team that had put me in the garbage, but a very welcome sight right now. "What happened, man? You stood us up!"

"There was a problem with the plane! I was stuck in Vegas—" I broke it off. What was the point of trying to explain it? "Where is everybody? Where am I supposed to go?"

He pointed at the distant spotlit stage and grinned. "These people are going to *love* you, man! Some of them have been camped out since last night to get a place up close!"

He could have helped me. He could have taken at least one suitcase on the thousand-mile journey to the front. But he didn't offer, and I sure wasn't going to ask. It's hard enough to win the respect of your coworkers as the new kid. And when they've already picked you up and heaved you into a New York City alley, you're not starting with much cred.

So I hefted my stuff and waded into the mob. If Woodstock had been about '60s peace and love, Concussed was about 21st-century do-it-to-him-before-he-does-it-to-you. I paid dearly for every inch of progress I made. Some of it was unintentional. A guy with mucho luggage makes a pretty big speed bump in the middle of all that slam dancing. Yet I was grateful for the suitcases. They took the majority of the blows that came my way.

Closer to the stage, the crush tightened up, and my progress stalled. People were packed in belly to belly, bouncing vertically, because there was no horizontal. The net effect of hundreds of tons of bodies leaping up and down in perfect unison was more like a force of nature than anything man-made.

I was stuck. Literally. There was no going forward, no going sideways, and no going back. If this had been Pompeii—a volcano preserving us in lava for all time—archaeologists would have driven themselves insane trying to figure what some tourist was doing there with luggage in the middle of a huge public event.

Then, with a spectacular crash that included the demolition of several guitars, Lethal Injection ended their performance. The crowd went berserk, and I was almost sandwiched to death between my suitcases.

To thank us for our warm reception, the band ripped off all their clothes and stood before us, stark naked except for long ski socks covering their privates. Bellowing insults and obscenities, they performed an impromptu conga line before stomping into the wings.

I knew I'd never have a better chance than this. I held my bags in front of me like a plow blade and began bulling my way forward. The fans shoved back and cursed me out, but at least I was making headway. I veered diagonally toward the side of the stage and arrived, more or less intact, just in time to see Cam roll up in a golf cart. He had driven outside the fence along a cinder track that ringed the festival grounds.

I was livid. "How come you made me fight my way through that crazy crowd?"

He leered. "Hazing, butt-wipe. You're the new guy. Get used to it."

There was no point in sulking. It was time for Leo Caraway to report for duty before he got any later. Purge was on next.

Backstage was almost as crowded as out front. Besides Purge, there were eight other bands, their managers, and their crews. They were all done for the day. The openers, the Stem Cells, had finished their set around one-thirty. But they had returned to watch history in the making. Concussed's full contingent of staff, talent, and crew was there, along with reporters, photographers, and an assortment of VIPs. This next set represented the resurrection of Purge after sixteen years. It was very big stuff.

Still carrying my luggage, I ran around looking for King, and finally came face-to-face with him in the wings.

"I'm sorry!" I panted, out of breath from hauling my worldly possessions through an army of ravening beasts. "The plane broke down and we came from Vegas by bus! I got here as fast as I could—"

He looked at me with such utter ferocity that I was cut to pieces. Then he stalked away without so much as a single word. I'm not ashamed to admit that I almost lost it. What the hell was I doing three thousand miles away from home with this man?

Bernie came rushing up behind me. "Jeez, Leo, don't talk to him before he goes on! He'll rip your lungs out without ever knowing he did it!"

I stared at my biological father. He was now standing over by the lighting array, his murderous gaze raking an innocent sandbag with every bit as much rage as he'd just directed at me. It was the trademark King Maggot anger, as much a part of his wardrobe as his black leather jacket and the noose around his neck.

Feeling a little better, I explained to Bernie about my jinxed journey west.

"Don't sweat it, Cuz," he said soothingly. "This is earn-while-you-learn time for all of us. Just watch the guys set up onstage, see what plugs where. You'll get your feet wet soon enough." He looked at me with a wry smile. "And I guess we should find a place for those suitcases."

We stashed them on an equipment truck.

"You'll pick up the tricks of traveling light," he said kindly. "Did you know most bands use disposable underwear? They get onstage, sweat it up, and chuck it. No time for laundry on the road."

"Thanks, Bernie." I really meant it. Here he was, minutes away from his band's official comeback, taking the time to make me feel welcome. Bio-dad might have been scary and weird, but at least bio-cousin was a nice guy.

I found a spot in the wings and perched on a stack of amplifiers beside a music critic from the L.A. *Times*. The crowd was getting restless again. It was almost midnight, and everyone knew what was coming next.

When the stage lights finally went out, the clamor of anticipation drowned out the introduction: "Ladies and gentlemen—" Yeah, right. "Lockjaw recording artists—Purge!"

It was the last thing I heard clearly for about six days. The roar of approval from forty thousand throats came in perfect unison with a guitar chord so distorted, so loud that I felt it below the gum line. The drumbeats were jackhammers, one in each ear. The vibration of the bass went right to my innards and out the other side of me.

I didn't like this kind of music. I didn't even think it *was* music. Yet I could tell that Lethal

Injection had been a bunch of kids fooling around with instruments in someone's garage compared with the authority and power of Neb Nezzer, Zach Ratzenburger, and Max Plank.

It almost slipped my mind that there was another part of Purge.

And then the wrath of the gods was unleashed on that stage. The reaction of the audience to seeing King Maggot after sixteen long years was so explosive that I thought the former racetrack might tear itself loose from the crust of the earth and blast off into space.

I'd heard the CD; I'd studied the pictures, read the accounts of shows Purge had put on in their heyday. It was all nothing in the face of the spectacle that now assaulted my eyes and ears. I'd expected the noise and the seething onslaught of King's lyrics. But in a million years I couldn't have imagined it being so devastating. Not good, but—*impressive*.

You could say it was god-awful, but you couldn't say nothing much was happening here.

> *"No life on Mars, or so they say,*
> *But we'll destroy it anyway,*
> *Make it clean for the USA,*
> *And how 'bout Venus next . . . okay!"*

As King bawled their signature anthem, forty thousand throats screamed along with him:

> *"Bomb Mars now! Nuke Mars now!*
> *Just you wait and see,*
> *Bomb Mars now! Nuke Mars now!*
> *The new diplomacy . . ."*

I looked over at the music critic from the L.A. *Times*. She wasn't making notes. She was weeping. Her eyes never left the figure that rampaged across the stage.

Neither did mine. The thought that this was my father, that I shared an earlobe and DNA with this force of nature, made me dizzy. That, plus the fact that it was well after midnight, East Coast time, and I'd first arrived at JFK airport at five-thirty A.M. But that was a small detail, and three thousand miles was a modest commute, to arrive at this point—the actualization of my quest for the mystery factor inside Leo Caraway. For there was no doubt that I was witnessing, on that stage, McMurphy in its purest form.

I'd never understood how my staid, respectable mother could have been taken in by a punk rocker. Now it was as obvious as Isaac Newton and the apple: this guy had *gravity*. He was an irresistible force.

Unlike Lethal Injection, Purge didn't feel the need to curse out the audience all that much. King started off on a couple of political rants, but every time he opened his mouth, the brouhaha of agreement and adulation was so instantaneous and so loud that he couldn't be heard. It didn't really matter. His issues weren't exactly cutting edge. I heard him mention Grenada in there somewhere, which I think was some mini-war back in the '80s that lasted about fifteen seconds.

That aside, it didn't seem that Purge had lost any steam during their sixteen-year hiatus. Potbellies and receding Mohawks notwithstanding, they were still the angriest band in America, capable of raising the roof in a place that didn't even have one.

The grand finale was "I Wanna Be Your Stalker," which, according to Melinda, had been the last song they'd recorded before the breakup.

Melinda. The thought of her brought a strange smile to my lips. God, she should see this! She'd probably be crying harder than the reporter, whose notebook was now blue-stained pulp.

Even I could tell that the band was building to a shattering crescendo. King Maggot took a running leap off the edge of the stage and launched himself spread-eagle into the frenzied crowd.

Drummer Max Plank pulled off a cymbal and Frisbee-ed it into a lighting array, taking out a three-thousand-watt flood in a shower of sparks. Zach Ratzenburger ripped all the strings off his electric bass, producing a squeal of feedback that was close to unbearable.

And Neb Nezzer hurled himself straight up in the air in his signature scissor-kick, landing on the stage in a full split.

I watched him, bug-eyed, counting off the seconds.

He didn't get up.

[13]

ONE OF THE LESSER KNOWN RESPONSI-
bilities of a roadie—it was my job to ride in the
ambulance with Neb, who was in a lot of pain, and
not taking it well.

"Just relax, sir," soothed the paramedic. "Tell
me what happened."

"I'll tell you what happened!" roared Neb,
temporarily the angriest member of Purge. "I'm
dying, and somebody's asking me stupid questions! That's what happened!"

I tried to be helpful. "He did a split and
couldn't get up. I'm pretty sure he has a bad back."

"It's not my back, it's my crotch!" he howled.
His agonized eyes focused on me for the first time.
"Who the hell are you? Do you work for me?"

The paramedic prodded Neb's abdomen and
got a caterwaul of protest for his trouble. "You do
that again," the patient promised, "you're a dead
man!"

"Sir, I have to find out what's wrong with you."

"Are you deaf?" Neb bellowed. "It's my crotch! It's broken! Sprained! Whatever!"

In emergency, the doctors discovered that Neb had been right all along. The problem really *was* his crotch. More specifically, somewhere during the leap/kick/split, the guitarist had popped a hernia that had become strangulated.

"But I used to do this all the time!" Neb protested. "It was my trademark back in the eighties!"

The doctor smiled patiently. "How many of us can still do all the things we did back in the eighties?"

While Neb was rushed into the operating room, I called the only number I had—Bernie McMurphy's cell.

"This better be good!" was his salutation.

"It's Leo." My voice was quavering. "Listen, Neb has a strangulated hernia. He just went into surgery."

There was dead silence, during which I heard music and laughing voices.

"Are you listening? Neb is having an operation. They're doing it *this minute!*"

"I'm thinking!" Bernie snapped. "A hernia. That's nothing, right? He's okay to go to San Francisco tomorrow?"

"It's strangulated!" I exclaimed. "The doctor says it'll take him weeks to recover."

A string of curses greeted this revelation. "First day of the tour, and we've got no guitarist. Why me?"

"It isn't you," I said reproachfully. "It's Neb."

He took a deep breath. "Okay, sit tight. I'm sending Cam over to pick you up. I'd come myself, but I've got to find a replacement guitarist, and they're all here at the party."

"Party?" I repeated. "Neb was carted away by ambulance, and you're *partying*?"

"You've got to understand, Cuz, in this gig, parties are like meetings. It's where a lot of business gets done." There was some feminine giggling at very close range, and Bernie mumbled, "Not now, babe. I gotta go."

"Is King at the party too?" I asked.

"He's not here." I couldn't tell if it was true or a manager's automatic reflex to protect his star. "Just keep an eye out for Cam. He'll be there soon. And listen, kid—good job. You stuck by Neb when he needed you most."

I was the only one.

Actually, I got to stick by Neb a lot longer than that, because Cam didn't show up. I was there when they wheeled Neb out of recovery at three

A.M. and established him in his own room. I was there when his eyelids fluttered open, and I heard his first words: "Do I know you?"

By five A.M., I was back in the waiting area at emergency. Cam had abandoned me, but I didn't care. I was finally asleep after twenty-seven frenetic, stress-packed hours, and it was plenty sweet.

A deluge of ice-cold beer soaked my face and chest, and shocked me awake. I jolted upward, arms and legs flailing. "Rise and shine, new guy. Been waiting long?"

Cam.

"Thanks to you," I told him.

He led me out to the parking lot to an equipment van full of roadies and girls. My anger dissipated enough for me to realize that they'd all been drinking since the show had ended more than four hours ago.

"I'll drive," I said firmly.

"You're the boss, Hoss," Cam sang out, dumping more beer, this time onto my shoes. But I stood my ground until he gave me the keys.

We drove around for a long time because nobody could remember where the Hilton was. I got directions at a gas station, and that's where we lost the girls. They went for frittatas at the Mexican diner across the street.

Finally, we found the hotel, and I dragged up to my room. Who dragged along with me? Cam, my roommate. Lucky me. At least my luggage was there, miracle of miracles.

Cam invited the others to come along, and I had to let them because I was the idiot who stopped for directions and cost them the girls.

"Well, okay," I said, "but I'm going to sleep."

They were loud and obnoxious, and pelted me with cashews from the minibar. I tried to be good-natured about it. Who wants to start something with all his coworkers on the very first day? I was caught between a rock and a hard place. What happened right now could set the tone for the whole summer. They were bigger than me, adults to my seventeen, worldly to my naive, and there were four of them and only one of me.

But when I saw Cam shaking up a fresh can of Budweiser, it was too much. I probably could have controlled myself. McMurphy, however, was another story.

My foot snapped up and booted the can out of his hand and across the room. "No more beer showers!" I snarled. "I've been taking your crap all night, and it ends here! I may be the new guy and the kid, but if you don't lay off, I swear to God I'll find a way to make you pay!"

127

I looked at their faces and knew I'd just made a big mistake. I wasn't sure exactly what they'd do to me, but this was about to get ugly.

And then there was a knock at the door.

"Later!" snapped Cam.

"Leo?"

Never did I think I'd be so glad to hear the voice of King Maggot. The mood changed in a heartbeat as all those Neanderthals broke their necks to let the boss inside.

King walked in, ignoring everybody else, and taking note of the sight I must have presented, having last seen to my grooming thirty hours earlier in Connecticut.

"You look terrible." A fine greeting from my bio-dad, for whom I'd crossed the country.

"I just got here," I explained.

He looked amazed. "What—now?"

"Bernie sent me to the hospital with Neb. You heard he's off the tour, right?"

He shrugged like I'd just told him we were out of Kleenex. "I came to see if you wanted to do breakfast. But I guess you'd better get some sleep." He turned back to the door and began to stroll out the way he'd strolled in. To the room in general, he said, "You guys are getting along okay, right?"

It was a question, an order, and a threat all rolled into one.

After a silent moment, I replied, "Oh, yeah, they're showing me the ropes."

"Good, because I promised I'd look out for you." And he was gone.

A big hulk I came to know as Julius spoke first. "Welcome aboard, kid. Good working with you."

I could have ratted them out, and they all knew it. I think I made some points there.

But not with Cam. When we were alone in the room, he looked at me and growled, "Who's King to you? Your daddy?"

I didn't say a word. I just flashed him my friendliest smile and crawled into bed, burrowing my McMurphy ear deep into the pillow.

[14]

MY NEWFOUND FRIENDS, THE ROADIES,
were driving to San Francisco with the equipment
trucks. King invited me to fly up with the band on
Neb's ticket, so we'd have a chance to spend some
time together.

And we did. In first class, no less. But it wasn't
exactly quality time. The life of a rock band on
tour was like boot camp. There were no thirty-
mile hikes or cleaning the toilet with your tooth-
brush. But every day was kind of an obstacle
course.

Autographs to sign in the hotel lobby; sharing
the limo ride with an interviewer. There was
always something to suck up every spare minute.
When we got to the airport, Max was waiting for
us with an enormous poodle on a leash.

"What the hell is *that* doing here?" Bernie
demanded.

"He's coming with us," the drummer said, and

you could tell by his tone that there was more to the story.

The manager was horrified. "You can't take a dog on tour!"

"I got stuck with him," Max explained. "Penelope dumped him with the desk clerk at six A.M. The proctologist is taking her to Rio for three weeks."

"Well, she's got to change her plans!" Bernie exploded.

"She's already gone!" cried Max. "Don't you get it? This *was* her plan—to stick me with Llama because she's pissed about the divorce."

"Find a kennel," Bernie ordered. "There are no poodles in punk. It doesn't fit the image."

Max didn't even hear him. "A hundred grand to redo the kitchen in a house I'm not even going to be allowed to live in anymore. Tiffany's shopping for grad schools. I'm going to be on the street!"

But, stressed as he was, Max dug in his heels and threatened to boycott the tour. With Neb already on ice, Purge couldn't afford to lose another original member. Pretty soon, Llama was being crammed into an animal carrier and loaded with the luggage. He howled all the way up the conveyor belt. As a matter of fact, we could still hear him in the belly of the plane, complaining throughout the trip.

"It could have been worse," was King's only comment. "He could have brought Penelope. She's louder."

We finally got airborne, but the business didn't end as LAX fell away beneath us. The minute the seat belt sign went off, Bernie took the floor.

"Okay, listen up. Pete Vukovich of the Stem Cells has agreed to stand in for Neb. He says he knows our stuff. I've arranged for rehearsal time tonight to bring him up to speed." He cleared his throat carefully. "What happened to Neb—it's too bad, but let it be a lesson to us. We're not twenty-five anymore. We've got to put on a good show, and do what we do. But let's know our limitations. We're none of us as young as we'd like to be." He grinned at me. "Except for Leo."

He turned to his bassist, who was double-fisting doughnuts from the hospitality cart. "And try to go easy on the eating, will you Zach?"

Zach was offended. "You're our manager, not our mother."

"I speak up for the interests of this band," Bernie said righteously. "Purge is a lean and hungry look. You're pushing the outer limits of that."

"Hey, I'm starving myself on the Richmond Hill diet—"

"Looks more like the Krispy Kreme diet," put in Max.

Zach waved one of his doughnuts in the air. "I budgeted for this. I was entitled to half a grapefruit for breakfast, and I skipped my carrot sticks from last night."

"That's some budget you've got there," King observed. "Like saving a nickel a week to buy a Ferrari."

"Don't take it so personally," Bernie told Zach. "Use common sense. That applies to all of us. Now, let's go over the media appearances for San Francisco. . . ."

When all that was finally done, I sat waiting for the father–son chat to begin. It never did. I cast a sideways glance at my bio-dad. He had his headphones on, and was as distant from me as he'd ever been.

Protestors surrounded the entrance to our San Francisco hotel.

It shook me up—two hundred sign-waving citizens—but King thought it was funny. "San Francisco," he commented. "This town never fails to turn up a few nut-jobs."

"But why are they bothering a band that hasn't recorded an album in sixteen years?" I asked him. "What about rap or something recent?"

King shrugged. "These people don't listen to music. They only know what *The O'Reilly Factor* tells them to hate."

The nut-jobs du jour were a group who called themselves the Society of Decency, or SOD for short. Their signs bore messages like MAGGOT IS AN INSECT and PURGE SHOULD BE PURGED.

As we walked past them from the limo to the hotel, they yelled and chanted at us. Some were singing hymns. We weren't in any danger. There were policemen keeping them behind barriers. But it was kind of spooky to have total strangers so mad at you. Yet it was the only time since I'd met King that I really had a sense that he was enjoying himself. He leaned into the crowd and uttered a Hannibal Lecter–like snake hiss that had people jumping backward for their lives.

A sign that read NEZZER = SATAN had a special attraction for Bernie. "Satan won't be coming today," he assured the woman, who was regarding him with distaste. "He has a hernia."

Llama the poodle, led by Max on a tight leash, chose that very moment to make a statement on the sidewalk. The reaction from the protestors was absolute bedlam. I honestly think SOD believed that Purge had deliberately trained the dog to do something disgusting.

By the time we were safely inside the lobby, we were on our hands and knees on the carpet. It was the first huge laugh I'd ever shared with King Maggot.

Max said it all. "And you guys wanted to put him in a kennel!"

No one could ever say that being a roadie is a cushy job. Amps and equipment weigh hundreds of pounds. The stuff is constantly being moved around, set up, struck down, and packed up again. Glamour? Try muscle aches, bruises, toe sprains, and electric shocks. The first time I plugged in Zach's bass, I got a jolt that had my hair standing straight up at attention. Julius claimed he actually saw a wisp of smoke coming out of the top of my head.

The festival had its own crew for the stage, the lighting, and the speaker towers. All the other equipment was the responsibility of the individual bands. And for Purge, that meant us.

Those were just our official duties. It was the gofer jobs that made this a twenty-four/seven affair: constant runs to the pharmacy for Advil and deodorant; walk the dog; pick the raisins out of the trail mix for Zach; put them back in for Max. Ever try to have a noose dry-cleaned? You get some pretty strange looks.

Max made me read the fine print on the faxes he received from his divorce lawyer because he was too proud to wear reading glasses. Zach had me sneaking him food, which was uncomfortable because Bernie had me spying on Zach to keep him on his diet.

The only band member I didn't have much to do with was King, the guy I was supposed to be getting to know. The other roadies were constantly shuttling him to interviews and TV appearances. I never got asked to go. Cam handed out most of the assignments, and he always saved the worst for me.

The travel was a lot less glamorous than it looked. Regardless of whether I was first-classing it with the band or trucking it with the roadies and equipment, the schedule was grueling. And with Cam as my roommate, even downtime was uptime. He was constantly on my case for being too slow or too inexperienced. Mostly, though, he complained that, "I'm never going to hook up with any babes with you latched on."

"Hey," I kept telling him, "you're not my

personal chaperone. Feel free to go girl-hunting without me."

In Las Vegas, he decided to take me up on it. That was my first chance to take out my laptop. Gates was the only friend I'd told about Concussed, and he'd e-mailed to ask how the tour was going. I was sort of hoping to hear from Melinda, but I knew I didn't really deserve it. Leaving town without telling her probably wasn't the best way to defuse the awkwardness that had developed between us.

I couldn't resist visiting Graffiti-Wall.usa and checking up on The World According to Kafka-Dreams. Actually, her message board was sparser than usual, but I did find this current posting:

> Keep an eye on the people you're close to —
> they're the ones who'll surprise you, and I
> DON'T mean in a good way. It's the friends
> you've known forever—THAT's where the
> stink's going to come from. P.S.—Speaking of
> stink—what's up with rest stop bathrooms?
> KafkaDreams seal of disapproval.

"The friends you've known forever. . . ." Was she talking about *me*? Who else could it have been? Not Owen, her personal shadow. They didn't start hanging out until high school. *I* was the one who went back to prehistory with her.

Perfect—Melinda was trashing me on the Internet, figuring that I'd never see it. It was almost as if she was accusing me of stabbing her in the back by having King as a father. How did that make sense? Nobody controls his own parentage. By definition, it's something that happens before you're born.

Anger flared in my gut. Did she think a genetic hitchhiker was like one of her tattoos or piercings—a style statement? Of all the potential bio-dads in the world, she had to know that I would have picked King Maggot dead last. My opinion of punk rock was no mystery to her.

And just as suddenly, the burn receded as my thoughts traveled back to that day on the commuter platform. I used to be one father up on Melinda. Now I was two—and the guy was her hero.

She had no right to blame me. But at that moment, I sympathized. I always sympathized with Melinda where dads were concerned. How could I not?

The P.S. made me frown. Rest stop bathrooms? What was that supposed to mean?

I shut down my laptop, and sat in the silence of

the darkened hotel room. T-shirts and underwear were already strewn across the furniture, although we had only been in Vegas for a few hours. Maid service was as important to rock and roll as electric guitars and record companies.

All at once, the isolation came crushing down on me. I had never felt so disconnected from my regular life.

Bernie put Cam in charge of picking up Pete Vukovich after his opening set with the Stem Cells and driving him back to the hotel to rest up for his stint with Purge that same night. But in Vegas, he pushed the job off on me. I found out why when I got into the rental van. Whoever had driven it last had left the tank a thimbleful away from dead empty. And Cam was too lazy to fill it up.

I drove to the festival grounds, so low on fuel that the motor stalled out on every upgrade. But there was no time to stop at a gas station. Cam hadn't given me much warning, and I didn't want to keep Pete waiting. The buzz was he was doing a spectacular job filling in for Neb, and Purge loved him. Melinda was right. He was the rising star of punk.

Concussed provided a luxury trailer for the performers to use as a dressing room/crash pad while on site. That's where I found the rising star—flaked out on the overstuffed couch, naked from the waist up, with four girls from the audience rubbing baby oil into his chest and shoulders. Did this guy own a shirt?

I cleared my throat, and Pete acknowledged me. "Get lost."

"I'm here to take you back to the hotel."

"Wait outside, yo," he mumbled.

"King asked me to make sure you're well rested for the set tonight," I lied. "I'd hate to let him down."

He sat up and peered through the girls at me. The musicians of the Concussed festival were a motley lot who belonged on Yu-Gi-Oh cards more than any concert stage. But they had one thing in common—total worship of King Maggot.

"Yeah, okay." He swung his legs to the floor. "Rain check, ladies. Gotta fly."

Still shirtless, he followed me out through the backstage gate to the van.

It took several tries to start the engine. "We have to stop for gas on the way," I said apologetically.

We shuddered into a Mobil station on fumes alone. Pete went to the bathroom while I pumped thirty gallons into the van. I pocketed my receipts and climbed in behind the wheel to wait for him.

Ten minutes passed. Then twenty. How long did it take to go to the bathroom?

Feeling half-anxious, half-stupid, I walked around the back and tapped tentatively on the men's room door. "Pete?" I called. Louder, "Pete?"

No reply.

Well, what would you have done? Jim Morrison, Kurt Cobain, Tupac Shakur—how many recording artists had died under weird circumstances over the years? I threw open the door and burst inside.

Pete knelt on the slimy cement floor, bent over a none-too-clean toilet. The seat cover was down. A long stripe of white powder had been painstakingly formed on top of it.

I may have been a Republican Goody Two-shoes, but I knew what cocaine looked like. "Hey—"

And then a gust of wind swept in from outside, and the stuff was airborne. A translucent cloud filled the bathroom. Pete reached out with both arms as if he thought he could somehow corral the powder and wrestle it back onto the toilet seat.

I tried to stammer an apology. Before I could finish, his bony fist was hurtling toward my face. I dodged the punch, mind reeling. What would the roadie's handbook say about this? We served at the pleasure of the performers, but surely that didn't mean we had to let them beat the crap out of us.

Not knowing what else to do, I grabbed him in a bear hug, imprisoning his arms against his sides. I was surprised at how easy it was to subdue him. Onstage, he seemed lean and powerful, a tight weave of knotted muscles. But in reality, he was just skinny and weak.

"That was four hundred bucks worth of blow!" he thundered, struggling against me.

"Sorry," I panted, holding on for dear life.

He stomped on my foot, causing me to relax my grip. I jumped back to avoid his flailing elbows.

"You owe me four C's, man!" he snarled, and stormed away.

I couldn't stop trembling. I had scuffled—physically—with a band member. My summer was over. I would be fired, sent home. My relationship with King Maggot would end here and now. And Harvard—

It took the loud honking of a horn to get me out of the bathroom. Pete was in the passenger seat of the van, looking impatient. "Hurry up, yo," he called. "You want to get something to eat? I'm starving!"

* * *

By the time I noticed the DO NOT DISTURB sign, I
had already been pounding on the door of Bernie's
hotel suite for several seconds.

"Yeah?" came a noncommittal voice from
inside the room.

"Bernie, it's me. Leo."

"Can it wait?"

"It's Pete. He's—" I dropped my voice even as I
strained to project through the closed door. "He's
on drugs."

I wasn't normally a tattletale. But sitting in the
restaurant sharing a pizza with a guy who had
tried to rearrange my face just a few minutes
before, it suddenly occurred to me—I was an
employee of Purge. I had a responsibility to tell
the band their replacement guitarist was a coke-
head.

At last, Bernie appeared, wrapped in a white
hotel robe, and escorted me into the suite. He
looked awful—hair wild, skin raw and scratched.
His bleary eyes were so bloodshot he looked like
he had conjunctivitis.

There was a woman dressing hurriedly in the
bathroom. When she stepped out, clad in what
were obviously her clothes from last night, I saw
she was not much older than I was.

"Leo, meet . . ." His voice trailed off.

She blushed. "Kelly— Hi." To the manager, she said, "Got those passes for me, Bernie?"

He rummaged around in a briefcase, and handed her a stack of tickets, which she secreted away in her pocketbook. "See you backstage." She flitted out, happy as a lark.

I delivered my report. "Pete tried to get his nose around a pile of cocaine in a gas station bathroom."

He stifled a big yawn. "And?"

"And he's trouble. He'll O.D., or get busted, or do something nuts."

The manager seemed amused by this. "Such as?"

"He tried to kill me because the wind blew his coke away!"

"You seem uninjured."

"The guy's wacked! And just like that, he's fine again, dragging me out for pizza. He's unstable!"

I could read the look on Bernie's face. He had spent the '80s riding the mechanical bull of King's front-page antics. What could Pete do that would top driving a Harley through a plate glass window?

"I can see Pete freaked you out, and I'm sorry it happened. But remember—this is Pete's world, not yours. Drugs have always been part of it. Before Pete; before King; before the Beatles. It's on the sign: 'Sex and drugs and rock and roll.' "

He had a point. I was just a tourist in the music business. I had no right to change the rules to suit me. Even Mom had mentioned it, one of the few details she'd ever provided of the encounter that had brought me into being: ". . . and there were—drugs." These were fast people—cavity-search people, although I couldn't have known that at the time.

"Thanks, Bernie. Sorry to come busting in on you." It wasn't hard to guess the manager's favorite tine on the sex/drugs/rock and roll trident.

"Anytime, Cuz. Hey, what were you doing with Pete in the first place? Isn't that Cam's gig?"

Uh-oh. "He got busy with some—uh—other work—"

Bernie wasn't buying it. "Tell him to stop by and see me, will you?"

My roommate was going to love me more than ever.

[15]

THE RADIO CLICKED ON, BLASTING ME
back to consciousness with the pounding
onslaught of punk guitar. Rubbing my eyes, I was
surprised to recognize the song—Chemical Ali's
set opener, "Rigor Mantis."

The digital readout on the clock came into
bleary focus. 10:02.

10:02? That was impossible! Cam set the alarm
for eight! We were supposed to be leaving for
Phoenix at nine-thirty!

"Cam, wake up!"

I was alone in the hotel room. Cam's stuff was
packed and gone.

That jerk! He had deliberately changed the
alarm so that I'd miss my ride to Phoenix. It was
his revenge for catching flak from Bernie over the
thing with Pete.

I called Bernie's room, but I already knew it was
too late. By now, the band was at Madame

Tussauds, attending the unveiling of their wax likenesses. They were heading straight to the airport from there.

Frantic, I threw on clothes, crammed my stuff into my suitcases and backpack, and rushed downstairs. What an idiot I was to trust Cam! It was no secret that he hated me.

I stuck my head into the restaurant in the hope that one of the other bands' crews had been delayed, and I could catch a ride with them. No such luck. The reality of my predicament was starting to sink in. What could I do? Take a bus to Phoenix? That would look great—rolling into town hours after everybody else. It would only prove to King that bringing me on tour was a mistake.

There was one more chance. I ran out of the hotel and threw my bags into a taxi. "The fairgrounds!" I barked at the driver. Maybe I could hitch a ride on one of the Concussed trucks—the big semis that transported the stage setup and sound system.

As we pulled onto the festival site, my heart sank. The speaker towers were gone, the stage and lighting arrays dismantled. There were no eighteen-wheelers, only the cars and vans in the campground across the way. This was home to the die-hard fans who were living on the road, following Concussed from city to city, criss-crossing the country in a summer blitz of punk and Porta Potties. And if the Concussed band members were a bizarre collection, their zealots were extraterrestrials. Picture several thousand headbangers living in tents and rusty old vans, sweating their way through all-day outdoor concerts. The black hole of Calcutta with body piercing.

That's not to say everybody was bizarre. There were plenty of ordinary kids and young adults traveling with Concussed. The normal people seemed strangest of all—like *Leave It to Beaver* characters who had taken a wrong turn in the studio back lot, and had wandered onto the set of *Planet of the Apes.* My eyes fell on one preppy looking polo shirt in the bathroom line, surrounded by Mohawks and safety pins on all sides.

"Stop the car!" I bellowed.

The shocked driver slammed on the brakes, and the taxi fishtailed on the gravel lane.

Not possible. You don't travel twenty-five hundred miles from home to run into Owen Stevenson in a tent city outside Las Vegas.

I stuck my head out the window of the cab. "Owen!" I bellowed. "Over here!"

He spotted me and goggled. It must have looked to him as if I had taken a taxi all the way from Connecticut.

God forgive me, I was happy to see the guy. His superior expression and nit-picking eyes, scanning me for flaws, brought back memories of my childhood—which seemed, at this point, about a thousand years in the past.

"Hey, Leo! What are you doing here? Mel's going to freak out when she sees you."

"Melinda's here too?"

"That's our summer," Owen explained. "We're following Concussed. We're going to hit fifteen cities if the Subaru holds out."

Rest stop bathrooms. KafkaDreams was on the road.

That meant they had a car.

I unloaded my luggage and paid off the cabbie. Owen let me carry both suitcases and the backpack through the unwashed crowd. Still, I have to say he seemed genuinely thrilled to see me, and blown away that I was traveling with Purge.

"That's awesome, Leo. What's it like?"

I thought it over. I had no idea what it was like. And Owen wasn't the guy who could put me in touch with my feelings.

"To be honest," I said finally, "it's a little

stressful right now. I overslept, and the crew left for Phoenix without me. Any chance of a lift?"

"Totally!" he exclaimed, amazed that I had to ask. "It'll be like old times."

I had no old times with Owen. I sort of had old times with Melinda, but that was overshadowed by the new times with Melinda. I wasn't her favorite person these days.

But she was glad to see me too. I guess in a far-flung, garbage strewn, broiling desert wilderness, any familiar face is a welcome sight.

Owen could hardly wait to break the news. "Mel, you won't believe this! Leo's a roadie for Purge!"

All the welcome instantly faded from her raccoonlike eyes. Sleeping in a tiny pup tent with very little in the way of sanitation around hadn't done much for her goth makeup.

"Lucky you," she said sarcastically. "Daddy hooked you up with a job in the family business."

Two dads to none, I reminded myself, swallowing an angry reply. I tried to reason with her. "Of all the things that aren't my fault, him being my father is top of the list. And don't call him Daddy. I don't."

"If you're with Purge," she said sulkily, "why do you need us to drive you?"

"I got my roommate in trouble, and this is his revenge. Can I ride with you guys or what?"

"You've got too much luggage," she accused.

Owen had an answer for that. "No problem. I've got bungee cords."

All the way to Phoenix, with the tent fabric flapping noisily against my suitcases on the roof, Owen peppered me with questions about life on the inside of the Concussed tour. He ate up my details about Neb's hernia, Max's poodle and divorce, Zach's diet, and what Pete Vukovich does in a gas station bathroom.

While I was telling him all this, it dawned on me that I was enjoying talking about it. I mean, *living* it was no fun. But it was cool to be the guy with all the great stories. Even more amazing, I was enjoying talking about it with Owen.

Maybe it was because if I hadn't been talking to Owen, I would have been talking to myself. With every juicy tidbit, I could see Melinda becoming more stiff-lipped, stiff-necked, and stiff-rumped behind the wheel.

"So you know Pete Vukovich, too," she said icily.

"What about King?" Owen enthused. "You've told us about everybody but him."

That was the thing. I was getting to know

everybody *except* King. I couldn't tell if his schedule was the problem, or if he was just avoiding me. It was probably a little of both. Either way, it wasn't something I wanted to discuss in an open forum.

"It's kind of personal. You know, meeting your—" The words caught in my throat. I'd been about to say *long-lost father* in front of someone whose father really was long lost.

Owen didn't press the point. He was happy to blab on and on about Concussed. Apparently, he and Melinda had always been planning to make it to a couple of East Coast shows. But when Purge had announced their comeback, the two had decided to follow the tour from city to city, until they ran out of either money or summer.

Owen smiled endearingly. "I guess it doesn't sound very Republican. But it's our last hurrah before college."

Ouch. It brought home my own predicament. When the summer was over, I wouldn't know King any better than I had when he was nothing more than a wild animal on a CD cover. Would I really be in a position to ask him to front me forty G's for college?

Aloud, I said, "The roadie life isn't very Republican either."

"I disagree," put in Melinda, who hadn't opened her mouth for the past fifty miles. "What could be more Republican than a cushy job going to the guy with the best connections? P.S.—we're stopping at the first Internet café we pass in Phoenix."

So that was how KafkaDreams was continuing her secret online life while living in a tent. "Well," I began, "I really shouldn't keep King waiting—"

"King waited seventeen years to learn that you even exist. He can chill out for another hour." Black-ringed eyes flashed at me in the rearview mirror.

It was after seven when we finally found our way to the campground where the Concussed nomads were setting up shop.

That was when I discovered I was traveling a little lighter than I'd expected. Somewhere between Las Vegas and here, one of my two big suitcases had parted company with the Subaru's roof rack at eighty miles per hour. Apparently, some of the IQ points that had disappeared since the days of Owen's 180 were the ones that carried a knowledge of bungee cords. A good half of my clothes were gone.

"You were due for a makeover anyway," was Owen's apology. I'll bet even *Queer Eye for the*

Straight Guy never thought of such a novel way to get rid of someone's outdated wardrobe.

Maybe I was just bitter because I now had no underwear.

What could I do? I thanked them for the ride.

[16]

PHOENIX WAS A SWEATBOX—A HIGH OF one hundred twelve. The city council begged Concussed to call off the festival, but the show went on anyway. The vendors ran out of bottled water halfway through Skatology's set. All day, paramedics were dragging people out of the crowd who were suffering from dehydration and heat-stroke.

The roadies were sweat-drenched and fighting among themselves. The band members were irri-table. I should have known from the beginning that something was going to happen.

I'd gotten Melinda and Owen backstage passes as a thank-you for dragging me and most of my stuff to Phoenix. I made a lot of points with them, particularly with Melinda. Even I thought back-stage was pretty cool, and I wasn't even a fan of this music. For Melinda, the chance to be behind the scenes, seeing the musicians close-up was

Disney World times fifty. And the gut-churning roar of a hundred thousand watts of punk at point-blank range was soothing to her soul. When King Maggot arrived sometime after sundown, I thought she was going to pass out. She wouldn't have been the first, even though the mercury had dipped to a moderate ninety-nine.

In the break between Lethal Injection and Purge, I got called away to where Max was personally supervising the unloading of his drum set. He hadn't allowed us to bring it over with the other equipment earlier in the day. He was getting really particular about his stuff. But his instructions to the roadies had nothing to do with drums.

"Never get married, you guys. It's like signing up for your own personal Saddam Hussein. Then, when she's through torturing you, she takes everything you've slaved for and runs off to Rio with some doctor who spends his days looking up people's butts, but is too blind to notice that hers is eight feet across. Poor slob. He'll be next."

Cam tried to be encouraging. "Max, you're a legend. You can do way better than Penelope."

"It was Halloween the night she walked out," he mumbled resentfully. "When I got home from the Masonic lodge, even the Tootsie Rolls were gone."

The heat was an accelerant for many incendiary tempers. Bernie was snapping at everybody, especially Zach, who was inhaling potato chips because "In this weather, you've got to fight salt depletion."

"Let's fight obesity first," the manager muttered, "and let salt depletion look after itself."

He was even snippy to the press, which was totally out of character. He normally made certain that all members of the media were welcomed with open arms. There was one reporter in particular—Rossi, from *Phoenix Nightlife Weekly*—who was pushing his luck backstage. There was an unwritten rule that newspeople didn't interfere with the bands and crew. But this guy Rossi couldn't seem to stay out of everybody's face.

"Listen," Bernie told him, "the show isn't a forum for your interview. We allow you to watch. It's a courtesy. And whatever you do, stay away from King. You don't want to get too close to him when he's preparing for a set."

Anyone else would have considered it friendly advice. To this bonehead Rossi, it was a challenge. He went up to King, who was in his preperformance mode, fingers steepled, preparing for the Vulcan mind meld.

"Hey, King. Chuck Rossi, *Phoenix Nightlife Weekly*—" At that point, the reporter's hand made contact with the Purge front man's shoulder.

The reaction was instantaneous. King wheeled and hit him with a haymaker that left an arc of burnt air behind it. The reporter went down like a ton of bricks and stayed down.

Bernie rolled his eyes in a here-we-go-again expression. "Flag the paramedics," he told Cam. "We've got another case of heatstroke."

I gawked. "But Bernie, his nose is bleeding! It could be broken!"

He nodded. "Poor guy hit the floor pretty hard."

I caught a glimpse of Melinda's face during all this. Rapture was the only way to describe it. I thought back to her project, "Poets of Rage." Among his other sterling qualities, King Maggot was known to have the hardest punch in punk. In Melinda's eyes, she was watching history being made.

So the full-frontal assault of "Bomb Mars Now" formed an apocalyptic sound track for the ambulance personnel as they loaded up Chuck Rossi.

If anything, the substitution of Pete Vukovich made Purge's music louder, rawer, and more explosive than ever before. In his hands, the Fender Stratocaster was practically alive. The once-venerated name of Neb Nezzer was hardly ever mentioned anymore.

But the heart and soul of Purge was still King. I'd wondered if the fact that he'd just put somebody in the hospital might affect my bio-dad onstage. Not a single iota.

Every time King picked up a microphone, it was like he had an exploding sun trapped inside him and the only way to let it out was by screaming. He was spectacular, devastating, tectonic. He was such a dynamic performer that he could get a 2006 audience all worked up about Grenada.

The Arizona crowd, parboiled by the heat, went berserk in their appreciation. Backstage, Owen was pumping his head hard enough to scramble the Connecticut Department of Education's most cherished brains. Beside him, Melinda was frozen in intense concentration, determined not to miss a single drumbeat, guitar riff, or caterwaul.

The progression of songs was becoming familiar by now: "Bomb Mars Now" led into "Filthy/ Ugly/Sick," followed by "Bored Ballistic," and "The Supreme Court Makes Me Barf." It was during the guitar solo in "Repo Momma" that they came. The cops.

You couldn't hear the sirens over the music, and the flashers were obscured by the strobes. But people got the idea when two uniformed officers stormed the stage, flanked King Maggot, and slapped a set of handcuffs on him. The microphone hit the stage, producing a blast of feedback that was every bit as musical as the song it interrupted.

There was a flash of pale skin and black clothing as Melinda Rapaport ran out and hurled herself onto the back of one of the arresting officers.

Well, I had to get her away from there, didn't I? She was attacking a cop. It was my fault she was on that stage to begin with. As I ran out into the lights, braving the barrage of spittle and clods of earth coming in from the audience, I found Owen running next to me. Between us, we managed to detach her from the cop and drag her kicking and screaming into the wings.

"*Gotta help King!*" she shrieked over the noise of the agitated crowd.

A few would-be rioters burst through the barriers and climbed onto the stage. But the arrival of several more officers brandishing billy clubs seemed to dampen their enthusiasm. It was too hot for civil disobedience.

King didn't resist arrest, but he wasn't going along quietly either. He made them drag him through the entire backstage area to a waiting squad car. I caught a glimpse of him as they ducked his head in through the rear door.

His expression was unreadable.

According to Bernie, everything was under control.

As soon as King had decked that reporter, the manager had made some cell phone inquiries, putting a local law firm on alert. They would probably be at the precinct house to greet King when he arrived.

I was distraught. "You *knew* this was going to happen?"

"This is how I spent the eighties, Cuz. You think this is the first time some pushy reporter came to and remembered who hit him?"

"I saw the whole thing," I insisted. "That reporter had it coming! I'll testify to that."

"There isn't going to be any testifying," Bernie told me. "Just stating names and releasing on bail. We'll get it all kicked long before a trial date can come up. That idiot Rossi only wants to see himself on TV."

I wasn't comforted. "Just let me ride with you to the police station."

He looked surprised. "I'm not going. That's

why we pay lawyers—so people like you and me can go back to the hotel and get some shut-eye."

So I went with him. But the promised shut-eye would not come. The hotel was built around a central atrium, and my window overlooked the front door. I sat there until three A.M., watching.

Cam came home, smelling faintly of beer, and combative as usual. "God, butt-wipe—how am I ever going to get any action if you're always sitting around here waiting for Santa Claus?"

"King still isn't back from the police station."

He looked at me pityingly. "Duh! They probably want him to spend the night in the can. The cops love doing that with celebrities."

I didn't like the sound of that. So I did what I should have done hours ago—I called Bernie.

He was not pleased to hear from me. "I'm going to start checking into hotels under an alias!"

I could hear female whispering in the background, which meant the manager wasn't getting any shut-eye either. If picking up women was so important to Cam, he needed to start hanging out with Bernie.

"King isn't back yet," I reported anxiously.

"Yeah, I know. They don't want to wake up a

judge, so he can't be arraigned until morning. Standard stuff—justice is blind, no special treatment, yada, yada, yada."

"You said he'd be back tonight," I protested.

"What difference does it make—tonight, tomorrow. It's already tomorrow. Go to bed." He hung up on me.

Completely agitated, I turned the TV on low. Nothing was going to disturb Cam, who lay on his bed, fully dressed, snoring like a buzz saw. CNN was running a documentary on covered bridges in Vermont. But on the scrolling headlines under "Entertainment," I read: "SHOCK ROCKER KING MAGGOT ARRESTED FOR ASSAULT IN AZ. COULD FACE 7 YRS IF CONVICTED."

I called Bernie again, and got the hotel's voice mail system. This was crazy! How could Bernie and Cam act like it was nothing when King could go to jail for seven years? Even if they didn't care about him as a person, weren't they worried about the tour? The band? Maybe Neb could be replaced, but never King.

The reason why Bernie and Cam were taking this so lightly was because King wasn't their father. But he was mine. Total stranger or not, he was entitled to my support.

I grabbed my wallet and headed for the taxi

line outside of the hotel.

"Where would the police take somebody to spend the night and be arraigned in the morning?" I asked the cabbie.

"Downtown—central booking."

It was a big, old stone building, more like an East Coast police station than what you'd expect in Phoenix. The runaround I got was reminiscent of big city police stations too. But of course, my experience was limited to cop shows on TV.

Either out of ignorance or police policy, nobody would tell me whether or not King was even being held there. But eventually, some clerk let on that a Marion X. McMurphy was slated to be arraigned in Courtroom 12 at nine A.M., just about four hours away.

McMurphy. A large part of my life had been dedicated to keeping McMurphy locked away. And now that somebody had actually done it, all I could think of was getting him out. A famous person wouldn't be safe in there with gang members and lowlifes. Or maybe the gang members and lowlifes were the ones who had to worry.

No. Not funny.

I didn't go back to the hotel. What would have been the point? I wouldn't have slept anyway. Instead, I found Courtroom 12 and parked myself in the hall outside, waiting for it to open. I passed the remainder of the night there, worrying and dozing. I might have gotten some decent rest, except three times passing cops woke me and patted me down for weapons.

"I'm waiting for my father's hearing," I explained myself to the third officer. "King Maggot, the singer."

He patted me down a second time.

All night, the place had been as quiet as a tomb. Around eight the next morning, people began to arrive. I thought it was the start of a normal workday. But by eight-thirty, the rest of the building was still quiet, and the hall outside Courtroom 12 was a zoo. Reporters, photographers, cameramen, sound people. The piece of real estate I'd had to myself for the past four hours had become ground zero for the next chapter of the Purge comeback saga.

It got so crowded that, if Bernie hadn't shown up with a battery of lawyers, I don't think I would have made it into Courtroom 12. Obviously, the Arizona judicial system doesn't believe in the principle of first come, first served.

They dragged it out, too. Every public nuisance and shoplifter, and a guy who exposed himself to a group of nuns, came up before the bailiff announced The People v. Marion McMurphy.

Camera flashes and floods lit the courtroom as brightly as the Concussed stage. Suddenly, there he was, my bio-dad, still dressed in leather and noose from last night, but otherwise looking as relaxed and well rested as I'd ever seen him.

The hearing was thirty seconds of mumbling and a gavel crack. King was released into the bosom of the media. I couldn't get near him. That didn't matter, because he never once glanced in my direction.

The judge wasn't thrilled about King using her courtroom to hold a press conference. So the media scrum oozed down the hall and out into the parking lot, like a giant amoeba with King, its nucleus, giving his usual smart-ass answers:

"Hey, King, how'd you knock him out with one punch?"

King leered. "Come closer, and I'll show you."

I sat on a hot concrete curbstone, watching from a distance. I felt like the biggest idiot on the face of the earth. Why would I sit up all night on a hard floor, worrying about King Maggot? What the hell was I thinking? That I had a special connection to this man? He barely even knew I was alive!

Eventually, the exhaustion and emotional upset

caught up with me, and I must have drifted into a light sleep. The next thing I knew, the reporters were gone, and someone was shaking me by the shoulder. I looked up to find King standing over me.

He said, "Are you coming?"

I swear, I almost told him I'd decided to call it quits and go back to Connecticut. That was the way I felt right then.

Instead, I got up and allowed him to lead me to the waiting limo.

"You look like *you're* the one who spent the night in the can," King commented.

"He did," Bernie supplied. "When we got here, we found him sitting outside the courtroom door."

King wheeled on his cousin. "What's the matter with you? We promised his old man we'd keep him away from things like this!"

The manager shrugged. "You want me to nail him to his bed?"

I spoke up. "On CNN they said you could get seven years—"

My voice broke. Not that I could actually cry over this. But I'd been on a roller coaster ever since I'd arrived at the L.A. airport—by bus— eleven hours late. I guess it all caught up with me at that one moment. I'd have given anything for them not to have noticed.

King stopped and scrutinized me. It was only a few seconds, but it felt like forever. I knew my cheeks were purple.

"A word to the wise," he told me, not unkindly. "Bernie and I, we know what we're doing. We were doing it before you were born. I'm not going to get seven years; I'm not going to get seven minutes. So when Bernie says don't sweat it, don't sweat it."

I nodded, thoroughly chastened.

As we climbed into the car, I distinctly heard King mutter to Bernie, "This kid actually gives a rat's ass what happens to me. Why don't you?"

Bernie laughed. "He wouldn't last five seconds in the rock and roll business. He's *nice!*"

I could feel my face burning again. If they knew my real reason for being on this tour, I wonder how nice they'd think I was.

[17]

I GOT BACK TO THE HOTEL JUST AS CAM was going down to meet the other roadies to divvy up assignments for the drive to Albuquerque.

"Be ready at eleven," he told me. "You wouldn't want to get left behind."

Thanks, Cam. I hope I get the chance to do something for you one day.

"Oh, yeah," he added in an offhand way. "Some bimbo called you six times last night."

Some bimbo? "You mean Melinda?"

"Didn't catch a name." He walked out, then stuck his head back in. "There was one clue. She said she was your mother. I told her you were in jail with King. That's okay, right?"

If I'd had a bazooka, he would have been a grease spot on the wall out there. Like my tenure with Concussed hadn't been stressful enough. Now he'd sicced my mother on me, arming her with information that amounted to a trifecta from

169

hell—out all night + in jail + with King Maggot.

I had called home a couple of times already, of course. That was part of the Concussed compromise. It's illogical, but I swear I could hear the jigsaw puzzles piling up on every available surface, choking out the inhabitants of our small home. The conversations were stiff and brief. Dad was dying to know if the issue of the tuition money had come up yet, but he was too proud to ask. And Mom was quiet because the Taj Mahal wasn't finished yet.

This morning, though, she wasn't distracted by any puzzle.

"What did that maniac do to you? Why were you in jail?"

"I wasn't, Mom." I tried to sound soothing. "I just went down there for King's hearing. It was no big deal."

"I think seven years in jail is a pretty big deal!" she retorted. "And if I was the judge, he'd get seventy!"

"Nobody's going to jail. It's just hype."

"I was a victim of that hype," she insisted. "A victim of that man. And now I have to stand by and watch him make a casualty of my son. Can't you see that this life isn't for you?"

She was right about the last part. I'd known it

at the St. Moritz Hotel before I'd even met King. But I also knew something else.

"I'm not coming home."

It wasn't just because of the money for Harvard, and certainly not because I thought the Concussed tour was so important. Yet it was something *real*. Most of my life, up to this point, had been training simulations. School, sports, the Young Republicans—even Harvard, if I got to go. How could I quit on the first real thing I'd ever been involved in?

"I don't understand you, Leo," Mom said coldly. "Why would you want to make that man a part of your life?"

Oh, how I was tempted to say it: *I didn't make him a part of my life, mother dear. You did.*

But I kept my mouth shut. Bernie was right—I really was nice.

That night, I got an e-mail from Gates:

> She's talking about you, right? What the hell's happening on that tour of yours?

It was accompanied by a link to the transcript of an online chat featuring KafkaDreams that was posted on Graffiti-Wall:

> KafkaDreams: Got into a fight with two Nazis
> and a Republican last night. . . .

I thought back to the onstage scrap. If I was the Republican, the "Nazis" could only be the two cops who had arrested King. The Phoenix Police Department would really appreciate that.

> BlondYossarian: Nazis, Republicans, what's the
> difference?
>
> KafkaDreams: Didn't fight the Republican—he
> was trying to haul me out of it.
>
> DarthLightning03: they think they own the world.
>
> KafkaDreams: He was just trying to keep me
> out of trouble. He's not a bad guy. If he had a
> heart, it would be in the right place. . . .
>
> BlondYossarian: Republicans have hearts?
>
> KafkaDreams: This one's only a jerk part-time. I
> give him a lot of grief, and he usually lets me.
> P.S.—He has royal blood.

Typical Melinda. Even when she says something nice, it still comes out as an insult.

So why wasn't I fuming?

* * *

If Purge had been punk's hard-living, bad boys in the '80s, that title today fell to the Stem Cells. As the Concussed juggernaut steamrolled past Albuquerque en route to Denver, I came to see that Pete Vukovich's extracurricular activities in that gas station bathroom were just the tip of the iceberg. The five Stem Cells, none of whom had yet turned twenty-one, had pledged wholehearted allegiance to the god of Bands Behaving Badly, led by Pete, who King described as having "a life expectancy of ten minutes ago."

High praise from someone who had once ridden a motorcycle through a plate glass window.

But to be fair, my bio-dad seemed less interested in the sex-and-drugs-and-rock-and-roll thing than anybody else on the tour. While Max, Zach, and Bernie etched maroon crescents below their middle-aged eyes trying to burn the candle at both ends with Pete and company, King never once went out clubbing or partying with them. Maybe he had gotten all the hell-raising out of his system in the '80s. He had certainly accomplished plenty of it back then. I was living proof of that.

Denver was Pete's hometown. Purge's guitarist pro tem was determined to play conquering hero.

He did interviews side by side with King himself. And when the sun dipped beneath the Rockies, he set out to cut a swath through the area nightspots stretching from Boulder to the south suburbs.

Pete led the way in his brand new Hummer sport-utility truck, overloaded with friends from his old high school. A stretch limo and two Concussed equipment vans completed our odd procession.

According to the Stem Cells, the hottest place in Denver was the Pretzel, a former downtown pretzel factory that had been made into a dance club and lounge. There were about three hundred people standing behind a velvet rope when we got there, but nobody gave that a second thought. For rock stars, waiting in line was as likely as a June blizzard.

A taxi squealed into the parking lot. I noticed a familiar head hanging out the back window, long tongue waving.

Bernie was disgusted. "Max, what's the mutt doing here?"

The drummer climbed out of the cab, leading Llama on a leash. "I couldn't leave him. He has acid reflux." He glared at Zach. "Why'd you have to bring those Fig Newtons to the rehearsal room?"

"Fig Newtons?" the manager wheeled on his

bassist. "How does *that* fit into your diet?"

"The dog's calories don't count against me," Zach explained reasonably.

Bernie signaled the taxi driver to hang on. "You've got to find a pet-sitter. You can't take an animal to a club."

Wrong. The Pretzel's management considered it an honor to host Max Plank's poodle.

Inside, the place was packed with gyrating bodies, Denver's beautiful people, dressed and semi-dressed to impress. The booming dance music felt dissonant and wrong after my nightly doses of Concussed.

Zach winced. "Sucks."

Amazingly, I found myself in agreement with him. I was no punk fan, but the dance stuff seemed canned by comparison. Just as loud, but more industrial, a computerized sound with a monotonous, room-shaking beat.

"Maybe we should go somewhere else," I suggested, shouting to be heard.

"*You* go somewhere else," retorted Bernie, indicating that the matter was closed.

The Pretzel was packed with beautiful women, more than a few of them gathered around Llama, rubbing the big poodle's belly and stroking his fur. I could see the wheels turning inside the manager's head. The dog was a chick magnet.

He ruffled his drummer's receding Mohawk. "Take a break, Max. I'll look after Llama for a while. You go have a good time."

In addition to Pete's friends, our group also included assorted Ball Peens and Hatchlings, a Dick Nixon, and a handful of roadies and crew. Pete acted like he owned the place, holding a clinic in Tequila Abuse 101 in the lounge area. Nearby, one of the old factory's original baking machines was still in working order, and clubbers helped themselves to fresh pretzels hot off the conveyor belt.

Go figure—in high school, warnings about peer pressure are constantly being hammered into your head. But Max and Zach, rock millionaires in their forties, couldn't resist trying to keep up with Pete and his friends. Within twenty minutes, Max had passed out on the couch, a glass still clutched in his trembling hand.

I shook him by the shoulder. He didn't stir.

"I'll find Bernie," I told Cam.

"*I'll* do it," Cam growled.

He wasn't being generous. My boss had another job in mind for me. Green-faced Zach had been scarfing down pretzels at light speed "to soak up the alcohol." It was my responsibility to find a discreet place for him to relieve himself of the contents of his stomach.

I managed to haul the staggering Zach out to the parking lot. The sight of him would have bleached Melinda's all-black wardrobe: the legendary bassist moaning and crawling around a patch of dandelions, trying to stick his finger far enough down his throat to make himself throw up. A member of Purge literally purging.

At last, he sat up. "I can't do it. Let's go back in."

I sighed. "Why don't we just call it a night?"

No way. He returned to the club, and I headed for the all-night pharmacy next door to buy him some Pepto-Bismol.

The next twist of fate: rock stars get special treatment, but I was no rock star. I was barred at the velvet rope for forty-five minutes, sorely tempted to chug the antacid myself. At long last, Mark Hatch spotted me and convinced the gate guardians to let me back in.

When I finally pushed my way to the table, Zach was into the pretzels again, and Max was awake, but just barely. Bernie was a short distance away on the couch, mauling a leggy blonde in a gold lamé outfit that appeared to be spray-painted on.

"Where's Llama?" I asked him.

"How should I know?" he mumbled without coming up for air.

"Who's got his leash?"

"Do I look like a dog-walker?"

"Well," I persisted, "you were the one who had him last—"

Bernie rolled away from the blonde and fixed me with a withering glare. "Beat it, Cuz."

That was when I caught sight of Llama. He was on the pretzel-making machine—standing on the conveyor, feasting on uncooked dough. His white fur shone as he passed through the glow of a spotlight, en route to the large hopper above—

The oven!

I vaulted over the back of the couch in a frantic rush to save the dog. Movement through the belly-to-belly crowd was like wading through chin-deep molasses. Angry clubbers shoved back when I tried to bull my way through to the machine.

Heart sinking, I realized I wasn't going to make it. In an act of desperation, I snatched up a small café table, sending ten-dollar drinks flying in all directions. People ducked as I hefted it over my head and flung it with all my might at the apparatus.

It bounced off the end of the belt, and lodged

in the hopper. Uncooked pretzels slid down the tabletop, piling up on the floor. Llama jumped down and disappeared into the crowd.

A hamlike hand grabbed me by the scruff of the collar, and I found myself staring at a huge round face that reminded me of a mean Charlie Brown. It was attached to a very large bouncer.

"It was the dog!" I tried to explain. "I had to save the dog!"

It might have gone very badly for me if Pete's friends hadn't chosen that moment to show the hometown hero that they could be bad boys, too.

Two of them jumped on the bouncer's back, flailing away at the Charlie Brown head. The rest followed them into battle, cheered on by Pete, who lifted not a finger in their aid.

Jammed with too many people for too many hours, the Pretzel was instant combustion. It wasn't a brawl, but we were packed in so tightly that every shove had a ripple effect clear across the club.

Someone pulled the fire alarm, but you couldn't hear it until the management cut the music. The place cleared out surprisingly quickly. I guess nobody wanted to be hanging around in case the cops showed up.

I don't know who drove the Hummer back to

the hotel, because Pete had to be carried inside. So did Max, and Zach was barely moving under his own power. I watched the limo and vans disgorging our group, and that was when it hit me—

Llama.

We had left him at the Pretzel.

"Bernie!"

"Shhhh!" he said sharply. "I see. I'm not blind, Cuz."

"You mean you *knew*? Why didn't you say something?"

The manager gestured in the direction of the blonde in the gold lamé, who had made the trip with us. "Anyway, Max wouldn't notice an air raid."

"He'll notice eventually," I argued. "Like when he wakes up, and there's no dog!"

"The club will get in touch with us," Bernie yawned. "Or the dogcatcher will. Sooner or later, the mutt will turn up."

"If an SUV doesn't run him over first!"

The manager shrugged. "That's an act of God."

"It's an act of *us*!" I argued. "We just jumped in the cars and flew. Llama must have been caught in the stampede somewhere. Nobody even looked for him."

"That's Max's problem."

"That's *your* problem," I countered. "Max is hanging by a thread as it is with all this divorce stuff. He's going to have a nervous breakdown, and you don't even care!"

"Shut up!"

It wasn't just what he said; it was how he said it. His good-natured, buddy-buddy exasperation had disappeared. Something had changed forever between Purge's manager and me.

"You little snot, I put up with your crap as a favor to King! If you work for me, you do what I say! And right now I'm telling you to *get lost!*"

The gold lamé beckoned. He collected her and headed for the elevator.

I stood there in the lobby, head spinning. Bernie would kill me if I bugged him again. Max was totally out of commission. Cam would never help me.

There was only one person I could call.

[18]

HE WASN'T REGISTERED UNDER MAGGOT,
so I tried McMurphy.

I woke him up. "Leo," King said groggily. "What's wrong? Are you okay?"

I just blurted it out. "The dog's gone."

"Huh?"

"Llama." I gave him the whole sob story of our misadventures at the Pretzel that night. "Max is catatonic. He doesn't even know it's happening."

"What does Bernie say?"

"Bernie's with a girl. He's out of the picture. Everybody's out of the picture. What should I do?"

There was dead silence on the phone, giving me a chance to reflect on the wisdom of disturbing King over this. This was the punk rebel who defined "attitude" for an entire decade. The man had refined not giving a damn into high art. He barely even noticed when Neb, cofounder of the band, had to drop out of the tour for emergency surgery. Why would he care about a lost poodle?

He said, "Let me have five minutes to get dressed."

I still didn't believe he was actually coming until he showed up in the lobby, a little unkempt, but seemingly not angry about being rousted out of bed. He tossed me the keys to one of the rental vans. "My license was revoked back in eighty-eight."

I was kind of nervous driving with him—almost like I was retaking my road test. When we got to the Pretzel, a scattering of cars remained in the lot. Some of the employees were still on hand. That was a good sign.

I banged on the locked door until one of the bartenders answered. Over her shoulder I could see staff and bouncers cleaning up debris and overturned furniture from tonight's festivities.

"Sorry to bother you. We're looking for a dog—"

She regarded me as if I had a cabbage for a head. "This is a club. No dogs allowed."

"It's Max Plank's dog," I explained. "He got lost when the fire alarm went off—"

Then her eyes fell on the man standing beside me.

"*King Maggot!*" she fairly shrieked. "Right? From Purge? Oh my God! Mick Jagger was here a couple of months ago, but this is way better!"

That was enough to draw everybody to the door.

"How's it going?" King acknowledged them with a casual wave. "Okay, cough up the pooch so we can all get some sleep."

The Pretzel turned out to be canine-free. A few of the staff remembered seeing the poodle in the club. But it had to be concluded that he had joined in the mad dash for the exits. He was out there somewhere, wandering the streets of Denver.

Llama was on the lam.

King wasn't the only one who got recognized. The bouncer with the Charlie Brown head glared at me. "Aren't you the kid who threw that table into the pretzel machine?"

"That was also because of the dog," I said quickly. "He was on the conveyor belt, and it was the only way to keep him out of the oven. Sorry."

"No problem," he grunted. If I hadn't been with King, I'll bet it would have been a problem.

Back in the van, I could feel my bio-dad's eyes boring into me. "You threw a table into a pretzel machine?"

I studied my sneakers. "Yeah."

"I didn't think you were the type," he said in an odd voice. "I guess destruction of property runs in the family, like the earlobe."

It was the most fatherly thing he'd ever said to me. I don't know why, but I felt warm all over. If I had burned down the building, he probably would have hugged me.

We decided to search the neighborhood, spiraling outward from the Pretzel in a widening perimeter.

"*Llama!*" Even yelling for a dog, King had an iconic punk voice, a piercing rasp full of what Melinda called the Three A's: Anger, Angst, and Anarchy.

"Llama!" My own effort was anemic by comparison.

"Come on, Leo, a real scream comes from your spleen. Listen—" He stuck his head and shoulders out the car window and unleashed a "*Llama!!!*" that lifted downtown Denver off its bedrock foundation.

A chorus of "Hey, pipe down!" and "Shut up, man!" rang out in the neighborhood around us.

He shrugged. "Critics. Okay, you try."

"I don't even know where my spleen is," I protested.

"It isn't rocket science, Leo. Just think about something that pisses you off and let fly."

That was easy. I conjured up a mental picture of graduation day—smug Borman at the dais, bragging about me getting into Harvard, knowing full well that my scholarship was history. I felt my spleen then, a deep wellspring of suppressed fury, a reservoir of pure McMurphy. The rage began to bubble over, the pressure building. It wasn't a question of yelling; I just had to loosen the valve:

"LLAMA!!!" It echoed off warehouses and offices.

He looked impressed. "We'll make a punk rocker out of you yet."

"Is that all there is to it?"

"You know what punk is? A bunch of no-talent guys who really, *really* want to be in a band. Nobody reads music, nobody plays the mandolin, and you're too dumb to write songs about mythology or Middle-earth. So what's your style? Three chords, cranked out fast and loud and distorted because your instruments are crap and you can't play them worth a damn. And you scream your lungs out to cover up the fact that you can't sing. It should suck, but here's the thing—it *doesn't*. Rock and roll can be so full of itself, but not this. It's simple and angry and raw."

I was wide-eyed. "That's how Purge started?" It didn't sound much like the version of events in Melinda's project.

"That's how *everybody* started," King assured me. "The Ramones, the Sex Pistols, X. Sure, we all got better musically. That comes with practice. But what makes it punk—that has to be there on day one."

I could picture King young and hungry like that. But Max, Zach, and Neb seemed like neurotic middle-aged guys, obsessed with personal issues, weight issues, and health issues. Not exactly what you'd expect of the Angriest Band in America.

"Back in the eighties," I ventured, "was the whole band, you know, like you?"

He didn't pretend to misunderstand. "You mean crazy? It's easy to be crazy when you're broke and starving. But it's hard to keep it up in a Benz. It's all about authenticity. The one thing you don't want to be in this business is a poser."

I remembered Dad using that word in the suite at the St. Moritz. Dad and bio-dad on the same page—the mind boggles. "Are you posing when you're onstage now?"

He thought it over. "It's just harder to *care* so much. In the old days, Reagan would do something, and I'd get so steamed I'd be ready to jump into the audience and start ripping off heads. Today, if the government does something I don't like, I know the sun's still going to rise tomorrow. It's fifty times tougher to get my energy level where it needs to be for a performance. I can still do it, but it wipes me out."

I gave him a crooked smile. "So the old King Maggot's gone forever?"

He looked tired. "Maybe I didn't get fat, bald, divorced, and herniated. But I'm just as middle-aged as the others. Still—" He flipped up his shades, and his dark eyes were gleaming, "I like to think that if something came along that was *really* worth caring about, I could get just as worked up as I used to in the eighties."

"That's why people with plate glass windows are nervous."

He groaned. "I barely remember that day. Everybody else does, though. The damn Harley has become an extension of my butt. That's rock and roll for you. Ozzy bit the head off a bat, and I rode a Harley through a window. And nobody's going to let either one of us forget it."

It's funny, I'd always thought of Purge's antics as vandalism, drug-induced insanity, and publicity stunts. Never in a million years would it have occurred to me that it had anything to do with *caring*. Not that I wanted to ride a chopper through a window, but suddenly my own life seemed very blah. I couldn't imagine feeling that strongly about something.

"It must have been amazing," I said wistfully.

"The hospital said I broke the record for stitches."

"Not the injuries; the caring. You know, caring *that* much."

"I wasn't exactly Gandhi. Most of the time I just busted stuff up. I was usually high." He looked embarrassed. "That's not what you say when you're learning to be a father, is it?"

I pulled up short. Learning to be a father? Since when?

"Don't worry," I soothed. "I had plenty of chances to be a burnout before this summer. In high school, the drugs are there if you go looking for them. I was into other things."

"Like the Young Republicans?"

I stared at him. "How do you know about that?"

"I Googled you. That's my drug of choice these days. Bernie's got Viagra; I've got a laptop."

I pictured myself on Graffiti-Wall.usa, spying on Melinda's blog, while King was at his own computer in another part of the hotel. Father and son Web-surfing, another family trait like the earlobe. I was amazed. Not that he found me online—I knew that my name appeared on the Young Republicans' Web site. I just couldn't picture this punk icon keyboarding the words "Leo Caraway" in the search field.

"Did it say they kicked me out?"

"No kidding. Did they have a pretzel machine, too?"

I was treading perilously close to my real reason for being on Concussed. I gave him the expurgated version. "They said I helped this kid cheat on a test."

"Did you?"

"Depends on how you look at it. But the problem wasn't what happened. It was that I refused to help the assistant principal get the other guy kicked out of school."

His eyebrow shot up. "See, that doesn't sound very Republican."

"There's nothing wrong with hard work and personal responsibility," I said righteously. It was the beginning of a lecture I'd given to a lot of unbelievers, cribbed from a stump speech by Congressman DeLuca himself. But extolling The Common Sense Revolution to King Maggot? He was the opposite of common sense. He had built a legendary career on a foundation of chaos, gut impulse, and rage.

An awkward silence followed. It underscored the chasm that separated my bio-dad and me. A fruitless poodle search couldn't span that gap. Neither could the Golden Gate Bridge. I was still a Republican, and he was still a McMurphy.

We were literally saved by the dogcatcher. A panel truck came around the corner and parked in front of an all-night diner. The driver got out and went inside.

I stared at the lettering on the door. It read: CITY OF DENVER ANIMAL CONTROL.

Something in the back barked.

And then the Republican and McMurphy were grinning at each other.

"If that's Llama," King vowed, "I'm going to church."

I had to admit it was a pretty sweet piece of timing.

We got out of the van and approached the truck from behind. I joined my bio-dad at the small window in the rear door. Mesh pens lined both sides of the payload, five across and stacked three high. Only three of the thirty enclosures were occupied. There was a yappy mongrel, a strange-looking animal that appeared to be some kind of muskrat, and—fast asleep in the far cage, bottom level—

A large white poodle.

"Jackpot," said the front man of Purge.

The door was unlocked. We entered to a barrage of outraged barking from the mongrel.

"Hey, Llama," King greeted the poodle. "How's it going, boy?"

Llama opened a baleful eye and glared at us.

"Penelope trained him well," remarked my bio-dad. "He's got her personality, not just her good looks."

I decided to take the initiative. This was my errand of mercy. And as a Purge staffer, I couldn't let King get his microphone hand bitten off.

I flipped open the latch, grabbed Llama by the collar, and hustled him out of the truck, and over to the van. King threw open the cargo doors, and we pushed Llama inside. He promptly curled into a ball and went back to sleep.

Our smooth operation was interrupted by a booming voice: *"Hey—you can't take that animal!"*

Enter one very angry dogcatcher, his breakfast rudely interrupted.

We scrambled into the van and I gunned the motor. Much of the tread of our tires was transferred to the pavement as the rental screeched away.

I flew through central Denver, wheeling left

and right down anonymous streets, in a desperate bid to disappear fast. I sneaked a sideways look at King, who was practically cackling with exhilaration.

"What?" I demanded.

"My son, the Young Republican." He didn't seem entirely repulsed by the idea.

"*Ex*–Young Republican." And if Fleming Norwood knew about this, he'd probably blackball me again.

"You can slow down, Leo," King added. "They don't do high-speed chases in animal control."

It was getting light by the time we hauled Llama into the plush lobby of our hotel. After the late night at the Pretzel, I figured everyone would still be asleep. But Max sat at a table in the restaurant, feeding slabs of Belgian waffle to a large white poodle.

"'Morning," he called, sounding tired, but otherwise none the worse for wear. "Whose dog is that?"

What were the odds? Another poodle in the right place at the right time.

We had kidnapped the wrong dog.

"Yours," King told him.

"Nobody's like my Llama," the drummer enthused. "Can you believe he found his way back here? Just showed up at valet parking ten minutes ago."

"Congratulations," said his lead singer. "Now you've got a pair."

"You thought that was Llama?" Max was amazed. "Can't you see that's a bitch?"

King stifled a yawn. "Definitely." And he started for the elevator.

I was chagrined. "I'm so sorry, King. I never should have dragged you out of bed over this. I totally overstepped."

My bio-dad looked surprised. "Are you kidding? That's the best time I've had in years. But wake me before noon and you're a dead man."

The mirrored doors swallowed him up, leaving me standing there, hyperventilating.

Well, he didn't hate me. That was something.

Now what was I going to do with this dog?

DENVER, CO
(AMALGAMATED WIRE SERVICE):
City of Denver Animal Control denied earlier reports that a purebred poodle was stolen from one of its mobile units by two unidentified white male suspects while the officer had breakfast in a downtown luncheonette.

"We prefer to focus on positive developments," said a department spokesman, citing an upcoming series of public service announcements featuring Purge lead singer King Maggot.

[19]

THE STRESS OF HIS DIVORCE WAS
turning Max into an oddball. He refused to get on
the plane from Denver to Kansas City, opting
instead for an eleven-hour drive with Cam in the
equipment truck that held his beloved drum kit.

Not that I was complaining. I got to fly on
Max's first-class ticket. This burned Cam up no
end. "What about unloading the stuff?"

"I'll meet you guys at the fairgrounds in KC," I
promised.

It came straight from King, so there was no
point in arguing. By then, everybody on the tour
knew about my special status as Prince Maggot,
which set me apart from the other roadies. It was
seriously interfering with Cam's plan to treat me
like snail slime. I almost felt bad for the guy.
Anybody who spent so much time talking about
hooking up with women, but so little of actually
doing it had to be in a permanent foul mood.

Cam wasn't the only one getting snippy as Concussed continued east. Bernie was annoyed at having to smooth over the dognapping affair, and fly King back to Denver to record public service announcements. Zach was bristling because a smart-alecky reviewer had referred to him as Zach *Fatzenburger*. Now Bernie was threatening to hire a professional dietician ". . . for the health of the band."

Speaking of the health of the band, Purge had heard from Neb Nezzer, who was out of the hospital and recovering with his family. He said he'd be ready to rejoin Concussed for the European leg of the tour. That was the topic of discussion on the flight—how to tell Neb he was out of a job.

"Pete's the future," was Bernie's opinion.

The squabbling was widespread. The other three Stem Cells were grumbling that Pete was more interested in his temporary gig with Purge than his permanent one with them. All four Dick Nixons were staying at separate hotels. Chemical Ali had fired two managers; one in Vegas, and one in Phoenix. Skatology's lead singer stood accused of sending love notes to Mark Hatch's wife.

King shrugged it off. "Touring is a pressure cooker."

He was the one person who seemed immune to

the infighting. Just as he'd traded all-night partying for the World Wide Web, he held himself
aloof from the backbiting. Maybe it was because,
as the true superstar of Concussed, he could afford
to. But I was beginning to think it was because he
really was aloof.

Onstage, he was as ferocious as ever. At the
Kansas City show, the fury of his lyrics blew ripples
in the jumping crowd like straight-line winds
through a field of wheat. Knowing that it no longer
came naturally, I couldn't help but be impressed by
the ultimate professional plying his trade.

It was the part of the set where King launched
into his usual anachronistic harangue about President Reagan's invasion of Grenada. I frowned.
Something wasn't right. Sure, he was all wound up
and ranting. But this had nothing to do with the
'80s. What was he saying?

"*. . . fifteen thousand shares of Apple Computer!
. . . twenty-five thousand shares of Altria Group! . . .
seventeen thousand five hundred shares of Citibank
Financial! . . .*"

The heat of the Missouri summer turned ice-
cold. All at once, I realized where my bio-dad was
getting this new material. I recognized it instantly.

It was my mock stock portfolio from the Web site of the Young Republicans of East Brickfield Township High School.

"*This is all we care about!*" King howled. "*Corporations . . . money . . . profit!*"

How stupid I was to feel that we were finally connecting! To be *flattered* that he cared enough to look for me on the Web! And what had the search brought him? Not his long lost son, but new material to update his attack on President Reagan. I was the new Grenada.

I listened, stunned, as tens of thousands of throats bellowed their repudiation of my prizewinning portfolio. It was a *game*—a mildly interesting time-waster for a bunch of high school kids who followed the stock market. Yet right then, if King had pointed me out, I swear the crowd would have fallen on me and torn me to pieces. Such was the power of my bio-dad to incite a mob the size of an army.

The ultimate professional plying his trade.

As it turned out, I was a professional too. The fact that I was an employee of Purge was the only thing that kept me from walking out of there.

* * *

As we climbed out of the Sunbelt to St. Louis and Chicago, the audiences grew tougher. The novelty of warm weather had worn off, and the crowds expected something huge to make fourteen sweaty, often rainy, hours worthwhile. The pressure inevitably fell on Concussed's headliners. They delivered, but it was killing them. Maybe twenty-year-old Pete could coke himself up into the Energizer Bunny, but Zach and Max were ready to drop. And although he showed it less, I could tell the tour was taking a lot out of King, too.

Melinda exemplified the new audience tone—still worshipful, but God help the band that disappointed her.

KafkaDreams:

> Mark Hatch has pierced his nose so many times that the cartilage is gone and he can't sing anymore. During the primal scream solo in "Pus," he had to stop for breath. What a poser! It isn't primal if you have to take two shots at it. . . .

I hadn't seen her since that searing night when Owen and I had pulled her off one of Phoenix's finest. My info came from Graffiti-Wall, and from

Owen, who stopped by a few times to say hi, and to mooch free food from the backstage catering spread. He was probably on a mission from Melinda herself, since he always made a point of mentioning that she was still mad at me for preventing her from protecting King. She had no way of knowing that I'd already seen my semi-forgiveness online.

"The two of us probably saved her a night in jail," I grumbled. "How come I'm in the dog-house, but nothing sticks to you? You were right there with me."

He shrugged. "Aw, you know Mel."

"No, I don't," I said honestly. "I've been hang-ing around the girl since the cradle, but I really don't have the faintest idea what might be going on inside her head."

"You've got to look at it from her perspective. King used to be hers. But how can being his fan compete with being his son?"

"That's only because she sets it up that way," I argued. "Me being his son doesn't change the music."

He shook his head. "You still don't get it."

As a peace offering, I wangled them backstage passes for the Milwaukee show. It was more a ges-ture of mercy than anything else. It had been pouring for a day and a half. The county park that was serving as the concert venue was a mud bog below a buzzing, churning cloud of insects. Pole-mounted bug-zappers ringed the stage on three sides. When the music wasn't playing, the sickening sizzle of fricasseeing creepies was pretty much continuous. Their tiny carcasses rained down like chimney soot.

The bands were pulling out all the stops today, pounding through explosive sets with a mixture of sympathy and respect. Only die-hard fanatics would brave such conditions for a concert.

By now, Max had evolved the simple process of setting up his drum kit into an advanced science. We had to treat his precious skins like spun crystal so he could beat the crap out of them during the show. Cam and I were the only roadies he trusted. Personally, I could have lived without the honor.

Thanks to that nightly time-waster, I didn't see Melinda until right before Purge went on. I almost dropped down dead at the sight of her. If she hadn't been standing next to Owen, I'm not sure I would have recognized her.

Two weeks of nomadic life had changed Melinda. She had either run out of, or stopped applying the pale makeup that gave her a ghostly appearance. Countless hours in an uncovered crowd, at the mercy of the sun, had tanned her a deep golden brown. She was no longer dyeing her hair, which was now growing out blond, and held back in a ponytail. Gone were the black flowing layers of clothing, ill suited to the heat and grime of the Concussed venues. Instead, she wore shorts and a tank top in funky counterpoint to her heavy black-and-chrome boots.

I couldn't keep from staring. *This* was Melinda, vampire of the 600-row of lockers? She looked *fantastic!* Even the nose ring kind of fit into the new style, an eclectic mix of Sex Pistols and the Gap.

She noticed my saucer-eyes. "You try coloring your hair in a Subaru."

"No—" I stammered. "You're—"

As I struggled for the right adjective, Concussed announced its headliners: *"Lockjaw recording artists—Purge!!"*

Awash in the blitzkrieg of "Bomb Mars Now," I decided it was time to introduce Melinda to King and the band. Owen, too. He'd been more of a friend than she had these past weeks. They weren't exactly my soul mates, but who was? Fleming Norwood? Would I fit in with the Young Republicans anymore, even if they hadn't given me the boot? I had become a displaced person—

detached from my old crowd, but not really a part of Concussed. Out here on the road, Melinda and Owen were the closest thing I had to a family.

King was normally pretty wiped after a performance, but he was nice to Melinda, and I was grateful.

"You look familiar. Didn't you get peeled off the back of a cop once?"

It was the first and last time I'd ever seen her gushing. "I've listened to *Texas School Book Suppository* at least five hundred times."

He favored her with one of his rare smiles. "And you haven't gone deaf?"

"Your music has saved my life," she said seriously. "I don't know if I could have made it without you. I own every note you've ever sung, even the bootleg recorded when you guys were in prison."

To my surprise, King kept the chitchat going. My bio-dad wasn't the type for small talk. He told me once that he had given so many pointless interviews over the years that he refused to waste his vocal cords on "white noise." When he had gleaned what he wanted from a conversation, he had no problem turning his back on you and walking away.

"Any plans for next year, Melinda?" he asked. "Going to college?"

In the weeks I'd known King, I could have counted the number of times he'd shown genuine interest in another human being on the fingers of one hand. What did he care about Melinda Rapaport's higher education?

It hit me—these were the questions you'd ask your son's *girlfriend*! I don't know what amazed me more—that he thought Melinda and I were together, or that he was acting like a real father.

King Maggot was a lot of things, but predictable was none of them.

He was also gracious to Owen, who, naturally, said the exact wrong thing: "I didn't think a guy like you would ever get old!"

The other band members took their lead from King, and even Bernie was friendly. The manager had been ice-cold to me since dognapping night. But he greeted Melinda and Owen like VIPs, and made a point of inviting them to the after-party being thrown by Citizen Rot's new record label.

Ersatz Records had taken a monster suite at the hotel, and the bash was a wild one. The whole scene was becoming a little old to me, but it was interesting to see it through Melinda's eyes. For her and Owen, this was a rare glimpse of the rock-and-roll lifestyle, and they had the ultimate tour guide. Bernie was taking the night off trawling for groupies to show them around.

"Hey, Daddy's Boy." Cam threw himself down on the couch next to me.

I already knew what his line was going to be. "Listen, Cam, if you find a girl tonight, just say the word. I promise I'll find someplace else to sleep—"

"Oh, sure," he said sarcastically. "The crown prince bunking on somebody's floor? You'll run crying to Pa*pa*." He accented the second syllable.

"That's bull, and you know it!" I was somewhat distracted to notice that Bernie was alone with Melinda. Owen had gone off to talk with Ylang Ylang and another one of the Ball Peens. "Have I ever used my relationship with King to get the better of you or anybody else?"

"Think you'd have this job if it wasn't for Daddy?" Cam challenged. "You know how long I spent wheeling cheap amps out of crappy airport hotels before I got this gig?"

He was getting belligerent, but I was totally focused on Bernie and Melinda. They were practically cheek to cheek as he pointed out the various punk celebrities around the room. It was the standard operating procedure I'd seen him use on a dozen girls over the course of the summer. His left arm had insinuated its way around her shoulders, and he "inadvertently" brushed her hair and neck as he made a point.

The manager hadn't passed on his womanizing to hang out with Melinda. Melinda *was* his womanizing!

[20]

I THOUGHT MY HEAD WAS GOING TO explode.

I had tried to avoid being judgmental about Bernie McMurphy's favorite leisure-time activity. And on some level, I'd always known that many of his nightly conquests had been more or less my age. But the fact that those girls had been *strangers* somehow made them seem more mature. As if hanging out with the backstage groupies and wannabes qualified you for the big, bad world.

Melinda had turned eighteen a couple of months ago. She was old enough to vote. She could join the Army and get shot at in strange and exotic places.

But she wasn't old enough for this.

Warning her with Bernie epoxied on would be tricky. I took a step toward them.

Cam grabbed my arm and wheeled me around. "Hey, I'm not finished with you yet!"

"Listen, Cam, if you've got a job for me, I'll do it. If you don't, get out of my face!" I sidestepped him, and strode determinedly on.

Owen jumped in front of me. "Who was *that*?"

"My immediate superior in the roadie hierarchy," I growled, not in the mood for his pestering. "Hey, what's the big idea leaving Melinda alone with Bernie?"

Owen shrugged. "He wanted to show her around."

"Bernie's always on the prowl!"

As if to prove me right, the two got up together, and the manager ushered her out of the suite.

I started after them, but Owen held me back. "She's a big girl."

"You don't know what he's like!"

"She won't thank you," he warned me.

I ran into the hall just in time to see the elevator doors close on them. I watched the indicator go up to twelve, the floor where our rooms were.

I was blown away by the depth of my emotion. She wasn't my sister; she wasn't my girlfriend. She had barely spoken a civil word to me in weeks! Owen had a point. This was none of my business. He knew better than anybody what it was like to have people sticking their holier-than-thou noses into your personal life.

I stormed back into the suite, a melon-size hunk of plutonium glowing in my stomach. And there was Owen, ready to put out the fire with a bucket of gasoline.

"I get it—you're jealous!"

I unloaded on him, not because he was wrong, but because he was *right*. There were a dozen reasons to be upset about Bernie and Melinda. But I was mad because I wanted her for myself.

I scorched that poor jerk with every ill that had been done to me since my McAllister scholarship had gone south. "You think it's my idea of a great summer job to grub around the country, getting my eardrums busted by a collection of bottom-feeders and lowlifes? You know why I'm here, loving every minute? Because of *you*!"

"Me?"

I'd kept it to myself for all these weeks, but in the flood of passion pouring out of me, it was impossible to hold anything back.

"I *used* to have a scholarship. But now I have to beg King for money because I lost it, thanks to you!"

He was stricken. "Lost it? How?"

"Remember the algebra test? Remember vectors? Borman tried to get me to say you cheated, and I wouldn't. So he made *me* the cheater. And cheaters don't get scholarships."

I stuck out my jaw and waited for Owen to tell me Harvard was overrated so I could kill him.

His face was ghostly white. "Why didn't you just tell Borman what he wanted to hear? I would have been okay."

"Yeah," I snorted, "you're *gifted*."

"I didn't have so much to *lose*."

"Easy to say that now—when it's too late!"

"I was *talking* to you, butt-wipe!" Cam again, red-hot steaming mad.

"I'm not ignoring you, Cam," I told him. "I've just got something else on my—"

"You don't turn your back on me! I'm still your boss—I don't care who your old man is!" He was right in my face, bawling me out at top volume in front of half of Concussed. Heads began to turn in our direction. I'd had more than my share of scrapes as an employee of Purge. But this was the first time I'd been forced to endure public humiliation.

My cheeks burned as he blasted away at me. *"You're too busy schmoozing Daddy to do any work! You don't know a standard jack from a DIN plug! You're hopeless when it comes to—"*

He never got to finish the thought, because at that moment, Owen stepped in front of me and delivered a sharp slap to Cam's face. "Relax!"

Hold it. Back up. Did I hallucinate that? No,

the evidence was right there—Owen's open hand, still frozen in the follow-through position. But why wasn't Cam on top of the guy, pounding him into applesauce?

Instead, the roadie just looked stunned. I was pretty stunned myself. In all these weeks, I'd never come close to handling Cam and his mean streak. But Owen Stevenson had managed it with a single, surgical smack.

Maybe he was gifted after all.

It was the last straw. On top of everything else, to be rescued by the likes of Owen—to owe him for what was left of my self-respect—that was the end.

I didn't wait around for the fireworks. I got the hell out of there.

I took the stairs all the way up to the twelfth floor.

Disaster—there was no other word for it. All the stewing combustibles in my overheated garage had gone kablooey at the same cataclysmic instant. I mean, Cam and me—that had always been destined to blow up at some point. But why would I suddenly spill the beans about Harvard after keeping it a secret for so long? How did it help anybody for Owen to know that?

And Melinda. Talk about something brewing

since forever. After seventeen years, I'd finally realized how I felt about her—just in time for it to be too late. I should have seen through the white makeup and black clothes. I had nothing but my own shallowness to blame. I should have paid attention when Gates had a crush on her. If he could scour the entire Internet and come up with KafkaDreams, then he could spot a pearl inside a goth.

Stupid, stupid, stupid.

During high school, Melinda and I had become as diametrically opposite as two people could possibly be. Yet never once had she abandoned me, even when I'd begged her to. What a loser I was. No, worse—pathetic. Now that she was out of reach, I was obsessing on her. I could even hear her voice rattling around my skull.

Then I really *did* hear her. I strained to listen. What was she saying?

"Come on, Bernie, I don't want to . . ."

Bernie's room! But what number? It would be a suite—those were usually at the end of the halls—

"I said *no* . . ."

The voice was getting quieter. Wrong way! My agitation growing, I pounded down the corridor.

"Please let go of me . . ."

Suite 1223!

Taking my lead from cop shows again, I hurled myself full-force into the door. One thing they don't tell you on TV is just how much it hurts to collide with a ninety-pound piece of solid oak. Luckily, the dead bolt wasn't set. The lock jarred open and I tumbled into the room.

It wasn't exactly the attempted date rape I'd been expecting. Bernie and Melinda were on the couch, with some kind of Purge scrapbook spread out on the coffee table. A wine bottle and two glasses sat there. They might have been struggling before, but now they had frozen, their arms still intertwined. They were staring at me as if I had just been assembled from glowing atoms à la *Star Trek*.

I scrambled up and bawled, "Let her go!"

"You mind your own business, Cuz—"

But I was beyond reason, beyond language, pure action. I kicked the coffee table out of the way, upending the wine, and sending the scrapbook and a pile of mail spilling out onto the carpet. I hauled off, and slammed my fist into the side of his face. Not being much of a fighter, I was amazed to feel solid contact. The force of the blow was enough to knock the manager over the armrest to the floor.

I reached out to take Melinda's wrist, but at

that moment, she came alive. I'll never forget the look of horrified loathing she shot me as she ran out the door.

Me. She was angrier at *me* than at Bernie. If there had been any lingering doubt that I had blown it with Melinda, it was surely gone now.

Bernie stood up, his brow a thundercloud over his rapidly swelling cheek. *"Get out of here!"* he rasped.

I turned and ran.

It was only after I hyperventilated my way into my own room that a clear picture of the mail on the floor presented itself in front of my eyes. Close-up on the logo in the upper left-hand corner of a business envelope: ALPHA DIAGNOSTIC LABORATORIES.

The DNA test.

[21]

AS A SPECIAL ADDED BONUS, I GOT TO wake up in the same room as Cam.

Not that I slept much. I was coming to see that insomnia was as integral a part of rock and roll as hearing loss. Although, in my case, the sleeplessness had less to do with music than my own imploding world.

The plan was to sneak out while my roommate was still unconscious. But he had grown sensitive to my furtive tiptoeing, and stirred with a subvocalized moan: "Ohhhh—did anybody get the license number of that truck?"

"Go back to sleep. You've got a couple of hours before we plow."

"I've got to cut down on the beer," he mumbled.

I frowned. I knew the difference between alcohol and a bad attitude. Cam hadn't been all that drunk in the hospitality suite. Why should he pretend to be? "Remember that guy Owen? You didn't beat him up after I left, right?" If Owen was in intensive care at the hands of my boss, Melinda would put the blame on me for sure. Not that she'd ever talk to me again. I was branded with the KafkaDreams Seal of Disapproval for life, thanks to last night.

"It's all a blur." His eyes never left me. "But I didn't scrap with anybody. I wouldn't forget something like that."

Thank God. "Don't sweat it, Cam. It was just another after-party. Standard stuff."

I wasn't being generous. I just had no time for the creep. The DNA test results had arrived, and the only thing between them and me was Bernie. Believe me, I wasn't thrilled with the idea of facing the manager just a few short hours after punching him out. But in a way, the timing was perfect. Now that the DNA information was in, the connection between King and me would be definite. The moment had finally come for me to come clean to my bio-dad and ask him to front me the money for Harvard. Then I could stop living this lie and quit the tour.

Funny. The thought of leaving Concussed— even with the money for college in my hot little hand—brought me zero pleasure. I was no punk rocker, nor would I ever be. Yet when I pictured myself back home with Mom and Dad, it all looked a little flat. There, I was the high school kid I'd been for the past four years. The entirety of my adult life had happened on the road with Purge.

But the matter of staying or going was academic at this point. No roadie, not even the lead singer's son, still had a job after decking the band's manager.

So I had a double purpose: get my test results and resign. From there, next stop: King. With any luck, Harvard would be my severance package. I wasn't asking for charity. It would be a loan. Dad and I would find a way to pay him back.

I hoped King wouldn't think this whole summer had been nothing more than a grab for his money, although it had certainly started that way. In spite of everything, I was glad I'd gotten to know my biological father. I'd come face-to-face with the McMurphy in my blood. And no, he wasn't perfect. In truth, he was pretty damn awful. But he had good points, too. He was an amazing man—a famous man.

A star.

Room 1223. Bernie's suite. The door was open, and the housekeeper was vacuuming.

"Bernie," I called over the noise of the machine. "Bernie, it's Leo. Can I come in?"

He wasn't there, and I wasn't sorry. I crept into the sitting room. The maid had picked up the strewn mail and placed it neatly on the coffee table.

I hesitated. It wasn't stealing. This was *mine*. Nobody had more right to it than me, except maybe King. And he was the guy I was going to show it to.

I found the envelope and noted that it had been opened. Exactly when was Bernie planning to share this with the people who were truly involved?

I stuffed the letter into my pocket and rushed out of the suite. Ducking into the stairwell, I sat down on the top step and unfolded the report.

There were several pages of comparative graphs and points of scientific methodology. But the final conclusion was contained in the covering letter.

The words stood out. They flamed.

> The genetic evidence indicates that Subject
> A and Subject B are not father and son.
> There is, however, a significant family
> relationship between the two specimens,

most likely that of second cousins or first cousins once removed.

Gravity reversed, very nearly sending me spinning off into space. It was as much a blow as the original McMurphy shock back in fourth grade. I wasn't Prince Maggot. King was not my father.

Oh, I was part of the family, all right. I had the McMurphy earlobe to prove it. But it didn't come from King.

It came from Bernie.

It was a revelation that absolutely blindsided me. Yet I should have known it from the start. My mother's tearful story of the night I was conceived—did that sound like King? Hardly. But I'd been watching Bernie hunt and gather young women from the moment I'd joined the tour. He used his position with Purge to dazzle them with glamour; he used King Maggot as bait; he was a predator. Last night the target had been Melinda. Eighteen years ago, it had been my mother.

So this was it—the moment that I knew for sure about McMurphy. And I couldn't even get that right.

I had the wrong McMurphy.

Suddenly, I was scrambling down the concrete stairs, all twelve flights to the lobby. If I'd been up on the roof, I probably would have launched myself into thin air. When you come upon something you truly can't live with, the first irrational instinct is to try to outrun it.

I blasted through the lobby and out onto the street. Downtown Milwaukee was alive, but I was in my own little world, in too much pain to notice my surroundings.

Shoppers and businessmen glanced at me curiously as I fled along the sidewalk, lost in my personal marathon to nowhere. Maybe on some level I believed there was a spot in this universe where a horrible thought like Bernie McMurphy being my father wasn't true. If such a place existed, I intended to find it.

I ran until there wasn't a step left in me, all over downtown, past churches, and stores and office buildings. And when I'd worn a layer of skin off the bottom of my feet, nothing had changed. I was still the son of a dirtbag.

All at once, I couldn't stand to be alone for one more second. I needed another human being, not for advice, or even companionship. I needed somebody to say, "Poor you," and agree with me that life sucks.

But who did I know in Milwaukee?

* * *

The taxi drove along the narrow lane that bisected the fairgrounds, separating last night's concert venue from the parking lot and camping area. Although it was no longer raining, the place that had housed an audience of thirty thousand yesterday was a mud puddle from the *Guinness Book of World Records*. The lineup of Concussed nomads waiting to get into the showers was a mile long.

This was my destination—this bog of huddled masses yearning to get clean. Not the showers, but a certain beat-up Subaru and the only two people who might care whether I lived or died.

Luckily, the tent city was breaking up as the tour moved on to Detroit, so the Subaru was easy to find. The pup tent was still up. There was no sign of Owen, but Melinda was there, in T-shirt, boxers, and biker boots, cramming duffle bags into the car's trunk.

She appeared a little tight-lipped, but not bad, considering what had happened last night. Actually, she'd never looked better to me, and it had nothing to do with her newfound attractiveness. Right then, she looked like home.

I could see the state I was in reflected in her horrified expression. I was expecting, "What do *you* want?" or "Get out of my face!" or maybe even a swift kick from those boots.

Instead, she asked, "Leo—what's wrong?"

I had no words. I closed the distance between us, wrapped my arms around her, and put my head on her shoulder. It was the most aggressive I'd ever been with a girl, yet it was no more sexual than a shipwrecked sailor clinging to a life preserver.

"Tell me what happened," she persisted.

To this day I still believe I kissed her just to get out of having to answer that question. Joined at the lips, we stood there, our feet sinking into the mud.

I was dizzy. Shouldn't there be rules governing how many twists a human being can absorb in such a short period of time? Kind of like the stock market curbs that kick in on volatile days? Yet, stopping was the last thing I had in mind. This moment had been brewing for a long time, and there was a fervor to it that reminded me of the steam buildup below a volcano's lava dome. Just hours ago, I was toe-jam to the girl. And now this.

"Hey, Mel," called an all-too-familiar voice. "I got the athlete's foot spray, but they were out of Gas-X—*whoa!*"

We jumped apart. It was such classic Owen timing that I had to laugh. And if Owen Stevenson could produce a laugh from me on this hideous day, he couldn't be all bad.

He spun on his heel and began to hurry away, his shoes making sucking sounds in the swamp. We chased after him.

"Come back," Melinda called. "It's okay."

He turned to face us. "Do you know how long I've been waiting for you two idiots to get together? It's about time."

"It's not like that," I insisted. "I just came to tell you guys—I quit the tour."

Melinda was horrified. "Because of last night?" She was instantly ready to blame herself. "Because of me?"

"You might as well both know," I said with resignation. "King isn't my father."

Owen was mystified. "You said it was definite. What about the McMurphy ear?"

My silence must have been answer enough. A look of awed understanding came over Melinda's face. "Oh, Leo—not Bernie!"

"Bernie doesn't have the ear," Owen protested.

The last time I explained something to Owen, it cost me my scholarship. I definitely wasn't going to get into recessive and dominant genes with the guy.

"Trust me. What Bernie tried to do to Melinda last night, he did to my mother eighteen years ago. That's the kind of pedigree I'm carrying around.

You can see why I have to get away from these people."

"I'll tie your stuff onto the car," Owen volunteered. I guess he forgot what happened last time.

I had a mental picture of my luggage, lying half-packed in the room I'd shared with Cam. "I'm not going back to that hotel. To hell with it."

"I'll get it for you," Owen promised, hopping into the Subaru. "It's the least I can do."

I was dismayed. "Look, Owen, losing my scholarship—that isn't your fault. It's Borman's fault. You don't have to be my slave."

In answer, he gunned the engine and drove off, spraying me with mud as a final gesture.

When I turned to Melinda, she was as pale as her former goth self.

"Your *scholarship*?"

I shrugged like it wasn't the catalyst that had set off a chain reaction of disasters that still hadn't ceased. With this latest blow—King not being my father—the dream of Harvard was pretty much dead and buried, for the foreseeable future anyway.

I said something absurdly brave. "Ivy makes me itch."

She was shattered. "It's *my* fault! I was the one who got you to tutor Owen!"

I was amazed. Melinda Rapaport was tough as nails. I'd seen her go head-to-head with goth-bashing football players, and it was usually the jocks who retreated with their tails between their legs. This was KafkaDreams, the anti-everything punk blogger with fans around the world logging in to see who or what would be the next target of her abundant wrath. Here she was, crying her eyes out—for *me*.

I pulled her close. "It's okay."

But she didn't take my word for it. She was hysterical. We were attracting attention from concerned neighbors. I knew a moment of real fear thinking that this could degenerate into a public spectacle. So I hustled her into the only privacy we had—the tent.

There, huddled in twenty-eight square feet, I took a stab at calming her. "Listen, Melinda—"

And suddenly, her mouth was pressed up against mine, and she was crawling on top of me.

I had assumed that nothing good could ever come out of losing Harvard.

I was wrong about that.

Owen was gone all day. I can't say I missed him, and not even for the usual reasons. He was being considerate, leaving us alone to give things a chance to happen between Melinda and me.

Owen's giftedness had never showed itself so clearly. He definitely understood more about the two of us than we'd ever guessed about ourselves. He may not have lived up to his potential to become the next Einstein, but he had a real shot at Dr. Phil.

Melinda and I didn't leave the tent in all that time except to go to the bathroom. We did come up for air long enough for her to apologize for being so weird back when it looked as if I was King's son. And I expressed my regrets at being such a stuffed shirt about her style and interests.

In a way, this moment had only become possible because I had been stripped of my Republicanism, and she had been stripped of her gothism, and we had somehow found each other in a campground outside Milwaukee.

Who could say how it was going to play out when we got back to our regular lives? But in this place, at this time, it seemed like destiny.

Owen finally showed up around seven, with my suitcase and duffle on the roof, and an extra-large pizza with the works. Leave it to him to like anchovies. Actually, Melinda and I were so hungry by this point that we would have started on the tent if food hadn't turned up.

"Owen," Melinda said shyly, "you didn't have to disappear all day like that."

"Oh, that was no problem. Besides," he added coyly, "I think I might have met somebody."

"*What?*" Melinda lifted six inches off the ground. "That should have been the first thing you said to me! Who?"

Owen just smiled knowingly and helped himself to another slice, folding it New York style.

She was horrified. "I've held your hand through a million horror stories! I *deserve* the details! P.S.—if you don't tell me, I'll carve it out of your entrails with my toenail clippers!"

Owen did something I've never been able to do under cross-examination from Melinda: he held firm. The guy was turning into my role model.

By that time the campsite was almost empty. Most of the nomads had moved on to the next city. Melinda and Owen decided to stay here another night. We would skip Detroit and catch up with the tour in Cleveland.

My own plans were a mystery, even to me. But for the time being, I was sticking with Melinda.

To sleep in twenty-eight square feet with two other people is to know how a sardine must feel. I spent the night scrunched onto my side, staring up at the canvas peak of the tent.

By now, Purge would know that I was a no-show. I wondered if anybody cared. Cam wouldn't miss me at all, and the feeling was definitely mutual. Zach would need another sucker to sneak him cupcakes and Doritos, but that was an easy vacancy to fill. Max wouldn't notice if I showed up headless in a tutu. All that mattered to him was his drums.

And Bernie. My "father." That really meant a lot to him! What was his first action when he knew the truth? To talk to me? Not on your life. It was business as usual for Bernie—another town, another show, another groupie. The manager had been growing to like me less and less as the summer progressed. Now that I was an embarrassment and a potential lawsuit to him, he probably hated my guts.

Sure, it crossed my mind to ask Bernie to supply the tuition for Harvard. For about three seconds. I'd lost pretty much everything, but I still had some pride. I wouldn't have taken that man's money to buy my last crust of bread.

My summer was officially over. In the sense that this whole experience was about getting to know my biological father, today was the day

I decided I didn't want to know him at all.

King was the father I wanted to get to know—that I *had* gotten to know, a little at least. I wanted *him* to miss me. He probably wouldn't. Now that he knew I wasn't his son, I was just an inconvenience that had muddied the waters of his comeback tour, a blip on the radar screen of his semiretirement. By Labor Day, he'd have forgotten I'd ever existed.

If only *I* could forget.

We took our time driving from Milwaukee to Cleveland. Outside Gary, Indiana, Melinda pulled into a high-tech rest stop that offered Internet access. I considered booting up my laptop to see if KafkaDreams was blogging about me, but I chickened out. I didn't let on that I knew about Graffiti-Wall.usa. I was depressed, not suicidal. Keeping secrets? Maybe. But she didn't tell me, and I didn't tell her, so that made us even.

At the Cleveland campground, we staked our claim to some prime real estate, right next to the bathroom station and showers. The Detroit show was still in full swing, so we were among the first to arrive.

In that city, Lethal Injection would be halfway through their set, stoking the crowd into a white-hot fever in anticipation of the Concussed headliners. Backstage, I knew King would be working up his nightly rage, so essential to his performance. I pictured Cam, running around, cursing me for skipping out on the work, leaving him sole nursemaid to Max's beloved kit.

I knew it would be coming soon—the opening power chords of "Bomb Mars Now." Die-hard Purge fans would imagine them as they had come off the guitar of Neb Nezzer. But I heard the Pete Vukovich version—raw, distorted, thrumming in my pancreas.

The issue of which riff would go down in history from now on would be decided in court. Earlier that day, we'd heard on the car radio that Neb was suing Purge for replacing him. Melinda and Owen talked of little else during the seven-hour drive.

That was the one Purge performance I'd missed all summer. And although I didn't want to be there, my absence felt wrong somehow.

I tightened my arm around the sleeping Melinda and tried to tune out Owen's juicy mouth breathing. After the adrenaline-charged atmosphere of the Concussed hotels, an empty campground in Cleveland seemed like a very lost and remote place to be.

Cleveland. The home of Detective Sergeant Ogrodnick of the Cleveland PD.

I didn't know it then, but I had entered the ZIP code of the cavity search.

[22]

THE EARLY BIRDS FROM DETROIT BEGAN
arriving late morning, and the nomads were in full
tailgate by lunch. Half a dozen hibachis were fired
up, with supermarket hot dogs sizzling on the grills.
I was amazed at the atmosphere of community that
prevailed among these punk fans. They looked like
something out of a house of horrors, but behaved as
if this was a '60s commune. Everything was shared,
there were no outsiders, and pass the ketchup. We
made s'mores over an open fire with a ska biker
gang from Des Moines that was collectively pierced
in more than a hundred places.

Fleming Norwood would have had a heart
attack at the thought of anybody who looked like
that existing outside of the penal system. I have to
admit to being a little surprised myself. But I genuinely enjoyed their company.

Later in the day, Owen, God bless him, made

himself scarce, giving Melinda and me a chance to make sure yesterday wasn't a fluke.

It wasn't.

It was starting to look as if I had a girlfriend—just in time for her to go away to college and for me to do what? Get a paper route? I could work with Dad in the hardware store, but it didn't exactly measure up to a full ride at Harvard.

The fact was every time I looked beyond a couple of days into the future, I saw nothing but smoke. I couldn't even decide if I should go to the Cleveland show tomorrow with Melinda and Owen. I kind of wanted to see King in action one last time. But the whole thing seemed too painful.

I didn't notice the commotion at first, just a distant hubbub when I awoke in the tent. Distant hubbubs were par for the course among the nomads, especially now that the campground was jam-packed. In a few hours, the Stem Cells would be kicking off the Cleveland concert. The battle for parking space had already given way to the battle for a good spot near the stage come showtime.

Melinda and Owen were gone. They'd mentioned something about grocery shopping this morning. I struggled into my jeans and crawled out of the tent. For once, the washroom had no lineup. Everybody seemed to be on the other side of the camp where a crowd was gathering, and the noise seemed to be getting louder.

When I came out of the men's room a few minutes later, it was a full-fledged mob.

"What's going on?" I yelled to one of the bikers I knew.

Underneath his glittering hardware, he was pink with excitement. "Hurry up, bro! King Maggot's in the camp!"

"Huh?" I followed him, my bare feet bruising on gravel and sharp stubble. "King? Here?"

King wasn't like Pete and some of the others who reveled in glad-handing with the fans. He once told me that the teeth-gnashing, blood-spitting vitriol of his public image couldn't be maintained up close and personal. It didn't make sense that he would put himself in the middle of thousands of punk worshippers. More than likely, this was an impersonator—a superfan dressed up as King in honor of today's show.

But then I saw him, stalking through the campsite like the Pied Piper, trailing rats in all directions. It really *was* King.

I could tell when he spotted me because he flipped up his shades and his eyes shot sparks. He closed the gap between us with deliberate strides and got right in my face. "Do you have any idea how many people are looking for you?" he demanded, cold with fury. "I ought to tear your head off!"

This caused a ripple of anticipation in the crowd. When King Maggot used a phrase like *tear your head off*, there was usually a head rolling around p.d.q.

I was thunderstruck. Why did King give a damn about where I was? He'd barely even noticed when his own guitarist crashed and burned five feet away from him. Why was he standing here chewing me out like he was my father?

"But King," I managed. "Bernie—"

"So you had a dustup with Bernie! So what? Bernie's a bastard! Who doesn't know that? You want to quit the tour? Fine! You come to *me*! You don't just drop off the radar, and nobody knows if you're dead or alive!"

"I—I didn't think you'd care," I stuttered.

His reaction was one of those gasket-blowing rants that had made him an icon of the '80s. *"What the hell are you talking about? What was the whole point of this summer? So I wasn't there to change diapers and put you on the school bus! I'm still your father—"*

He said more—a lot more, and at maximum decibelage, but I never got past those words: *I'm still your father.*

He didn't know! Bernie hadn't told him. That lowlife didn't want to take responsibility for being my father, so he let King go on thinking *he* was. Quite a family, those McMurphys. They treated each other just as badly as they treated everybody else.

King was still yelling. "Not to mention that I promised your old man you were safe with me! That wasn't bull! I *meant* that!" For someone with zero parenting experience, he really knew how to lay a guilt trip on a guy.

"Sorry, King," I mumbled. "I thought I was fired."

"Well, you're not. So what'll it be? Are you coming back or going home?"

I'm still not sure why I didn't tell him about the DNA test results. Some of it was definitely cowardice. I was surrounded by King's acolytes. And just as referees are subconsciously swayed to make calls in favor of the home team, I felt a strange pressure to give the nomads the happy ending they seemed to want.

But I have another theory, and I'm not proud of it. On some semiconscious level, I was thinking that, as long as King didn't know the truth, Harvard wasn't dead yet. And since Bernie wasn't going to spill the beans, my McMurphy ear and I might be able to keep the secret safe long enough to get the first year's tuition squared away.

"I'll come back," I told him, to the delight of the nomads. "I just have to write a note to Melinda."

I make this excuse: I was desperate.

Backstage at Concussed it was like I'd never left. Nobody asked, "Where were you?" They just gave me the crappiest jobs, and I did them. Business as usual.

Well, not exactly as usual. For one thing, Cam mumbled, "Good to see you, kid," which really floored me. Maybe King had threatened to tear *his* head off too.

Also not as usual, because Max had recruited Julius as the new nanny to his drums. I knew from experience what a pressure job that was. When Julius dropped the snare, Max threw the kind of hissy fit that you normally associate with toddlers and Tasmanian devils. For a minute there, I was afraid the drum might be broken. It made a funny rattling sound as it hit the floor. Luckily, though, Max pronounced it okay, which was the only reason Julius was permitted to go on living.

Bernie had made good on his threat to hire a nutritionist for Zach. Her name was Ariadne, and she looked more like a supermodel than a nutritionist—which probably explained how she wowed Bernie at the interview. It obviously wasn't for her skills as a dietician and motivator. Zach was presently working on a cinnamon bun the size of a curling stone, and she wasn't even looking in his direction.

Another unfamiliar face backstage—a lawyer with a ski-jump nose and a paper to serve that nobody would accept from him. We'd been briefed about this. He was a high-profile attorney hired by Neb Nezzer, who had taken out an injunction to stop Purge from performing without him. At least three times I watched the document flutter to the floor off Bernie's chest. According to the manager, even closing your hand on the paper constituted acceptance. And God help whoever did that.

Bernie had a circular black-and-yellow bruise on his left cheek. It had probably faded since I'd put it there four days ago.

He greeted me warily. "Cuz."

"I'm not your *cuz*," I told him. "I'm nothing to you."

"You're less than nothing to me," he confirmed. "If I had my way, you'd never come near this stage. Not without buying a ticket."

I glared at him. "Do you even remember my mother?"

He looked exasperated. "You have no idea what it was like to be with Purge in the eighties. Wall-to-wall chicks. You think I remember one any more than the others? We were crazy in those days."

"Sounds like you've really grown up since then," I muttered sarcastically.

"What do you want me to say?" he countered. "That she was a princess and I loved her dearly? You know how I am. Some people get into this business for the music or the money, or because they think they can change the world. I was always in it for the women. I never pretended to be anything else."

Charles Manson could have said the same thing about killing people.

Lethal Injection came crashing to their usual cacophonous ending, and the roar of the crowd gradually petered out into relative quiet.

The moment had arrived for the Lethal Injection roadies and us to strike down the old and put up the new. I'm not sure why, but somehow I knew that I was doing this for the last time. Was it instinct? Or maybe the unusually large number of uniformed police officers in and around the stage area?

Ski-Jump Nose was arguing with one of them, probably the commander, gesturing emphatically with his unserved court document. The cops couldn't do anything until someone accepted that injunction. Fat chance of finding anybody stupid enough to do that.

The lights went down to a buzz of super-charged excitement.

"Lockjaw recording artists—*Purge!*"

It might have been just me, but the sound seemed *bigger* tonight. Max's drums were a barrage, like a battlefield firefight. Zach's bass could be measured on the Richter scale. Pete's guitar roared out of the speaker towers with a ferocity that was almost scary.

And King. Maybe this wasn't the '80s anymore. Maybe rage was hard work now. But tonight he blazed ten feet tall across that stage, hurling fireballs with his vocals.

I drank it in, experiencing "Bomb Mars Now" as if hearing it for the first time. In a way, it *was* the first time, because I'd never really liked it before. I'd learned to appreciate things about it, but I hadn't allowed myself to experience the whole tableau. It was almost precious to me now, not just the music, but the whole thing—the lights, the fans, the night; the cocktail of musicians, instruments, and a hundred thousand watts of power, turning an empty field into a nuclear detonation of sound and fury.

It had taken all summer, but I had finally become a punk Republican, if not the first, then one of a select few.

My eyes wandered backstage where my fellow crew members were monitoring soundboards and mixers, and standing by to attend quickly to blown amps and broken guitar strings.

I blinked in surprise. What was Owen Stevenson doing in the wings? He didn't have a backstage pass for tonight. Instinctively, I looked around for Melinda. But it was just Owen, grooving to the music in the midst of a group of roadies. He saw me, waved, and started to walk over.

It unfolded like a bad pantomime. Owen took three steps before his path was blocked by Ski-Jump Nose. The lawyer held out the injunction to the one person who hadn't been told not to take it.

I yelled, "Owen—don't!" But he didn't have a hope of hearing me over "The Supreme Court Makes Me Barf."

He reached out and accepted the paper.

And all hell broke loose.

Ski-Jump Nose signaled the cops, and a sea of blue swarmed the stage. The speaker towers fairly exploded with the twanging thwack of a nightstick making contact with Pete's Stratocaster. Zach's bass hit the stage with a deep-throated *woomph!* Microphones went down in a shriek of feedback.

"*Hey!*" Bernie was wading into the melee. "That kid doesn't work for us! *We haven't been served!*"

In the audience, thirty thousand throats were screaming with outrage. A brave and foolhardy few were rushing the stage where they were met by more nightsticks.

In the midst of the chaos, burst Ariadne, Zach's nutritionist. I watched, dumbfounded, as she clicked open a pocketknife and ran out onto the stage.

"*No-o-o!!*" I cried in horror, and took off after her. What kind of dietician carried a switchblade? All I could think of was John Lennon being assassinated by a demented fan. What if this crazy woman was trying to get her name in the paper by stabbing King?

Heart thumping, I followed her through the sea of struggling people. She bulldozed her way to Max's kit, and, before I could stop her, she had slit open every drum in the set. I didn't think anything could bring order to that donnybrook. But the sight of a supermodel nutritionist carving up all those drums focused everyone's attention on the back of the stage. Max's demented scream helped.

Ariadne reached into the snare and pulled out a fistful of the most brilliant jewelry I'd ever seen. There were diamond necklaces, strings of pearls, chokers set with sapphires and rubies, and gold chains the thickness of hemp.

The cops took one look at this dragon's hoard of treasure and forgot all about Neb Nezzer and his little injunction.

I was twice as blown away as they were. I mean, had I missed something? A cache of hidden jewels?

What the hell was going on?

Purge was arrested. Not just the band. All of us— the manager, the staff, the roadies. We were interrogated and searched. That's how I came to meet Detective Sergeant Ogrodnick and his rubber glove.

So help me, I didn't even know what a cavity search was. And when the sergeant explained it, I'm not ashamed to admit I burst into tears.

"But why?" I bawled. "What are you looking for? What do you think I have up there? Drugs?"

"Sorry, son. Standard procedure when there's stolen jewelry involved."

"Stolen jewelry?" But of course that's what they'd think when a zillion dollars worth of gems comes out of a snare drum. For all they knew, Purge was a front for a roving band of cat burglars, using Concussed as a cover.

I won't go into specifics. I don't want to give the impression that it was bigger than it was. It wasn't ripped from the imagination of some sadistic Roman emperor. It was even over pretty fast. But I left that room a changed man. I was so upset, flustered, and discombobulated by the whole experience that I was actually relieved when Ogrodnick didn't pull at least a couple of earrings out of there.

The whole story came out after far too many hours and far too many anal probes. Neb Nezzer had nothing to do with our misfortune. It seemed that Ariadne wasn't a real dietician. She was a private investigator working for Penelope Plank. She'd been hired to smoke out where Max was hiding his money from her divorce lawyers. In the snare drum, as it turned out.

As Concussed moved from town to town, the drummer had been visiting pawnshops and jewelry stores, turning his life savings into gold and precious stones. In September, when the tour began its European leg, the loot would be shipped out of the country in Max's drum set, converted back into cash in Switzerland, and stashed in a numbered Swiss account.

When the Planks' assets were split in half in the settlement, most of Max's earnings from the '80s would be out of his estranged wife's reach.

Max confessed all this at about five A.M. in order to avoid his own cavity search. He even had the receipts back at the hotel to prove he was telling the truth.

The fact that he chose to spill his guts then, and not five hours earlier, thereby sparing the rest of us, was the reason Purge broke up that night.

Concussed would have to carry on without its headliner.

It happened right there in the police station. It was remarkably civilized, considering Purge's reputation. There was no yelling, no fisticuffs. King just turned to the others and said, "I don't want to do this anymore."

Bernie put up a fuss, citing loyalties, long friendships, and contractual obligations. But King *was* Purge. All the discussion back and forth was so much hot air.

"I'm just done," King insisted.

And the comeback was over.

It would have been sadder if the others had

disagreed with him more. But Neb was already gone, Zach was a middle-aged fat guy, and Max's heart was in divorce court, trying to put a good spin on this attempt to take the money and run.

The angriest band in America had lost interest in itself.

King and I shared a cab back to the hotel to pick up our stuff, and headed straight to the airport after that. He bought himself a ticket to L.A. and me one to New York.

He seemed to relax once our escape had been mapped out, and I'd called my parents to meet me at LaGuardia.

He leaned back on the couch in the VIP lounge. "Of all the cavity searches I've been through, I have to say this one ranks about sixth."

Back in Exam 3 with Detective Sergeant Ogrodnick, I had thought I'd never laugh again. I was relieved to be proven wrong so quickly.

He turned serious. "I'm sorry you had to go through that. Leave it to Max to put everybody in a meat grinder and pull back just in time to save his own carcass. I guess the summer didn't work out like we planned, huh?"

"I enjoyed it," I told him. "Not this last part, but—" Suddenly, I couldn't come up with anything to list. So I told the truth. "Getting to know you is something I'll always remember."

He nodded gravely. "Same here. Listen, Leo, I know you've already got a family. But never forget I'm your father. If you ever need anything—anything—I'm just a phone call away."

I gawked at him. This was it—Harvard on a silver platter. I didn't even have to bring up the subject. He'd handed me the opening. All I needed to do was say the words, and I was home free.

My mouth was made of stone, sealing the sentence inside my head. I sat facing him, unable to speak as the PA system announced the boarding of my flight. In a few minutes, I'd be on that plane, and the chance would be gone forever. The time to speak was *now*.

I couldn't do it. Maybe I didn't have the guts to tell him about the DNA test, but I wasn't going to take his money based on a lie. The thought that I'd even considered it made my face burn in shame.

I leaped to my feet. It was the only way I could manage to hold it together. Warts and all, Marion X. McMurphy was the most genuine person who had ever touched my life. And what had I contributed to our relationship? Conniving. Deception. Greed.

"I don't deserve a father like you!" I blurted, and ran for the gate.

[23]

PURGE'S BREAKUP AND DEPARTURE FROM
Concussed made front-page news all across the
country. An estimated 3.5 million dollars in gold
and gemstones featured prominently in the story.
If Max had been hoping to keep the incident from
reaching his divorce court judge, he was out of
luck.

The role of Detective Sergeant Ogrodnick in
the incident was not considered newsworthy—
except in my lingering nightmares.

Punk fans were devastated, especially those in
the East and in Europe, who had been eagerly
awaiting the arrival of King Maggot and Purge.

The Concussed festival's organizers, however,
had managed to take these lemons and make
lemonade. They had quickly signed the surviving
members of the Sex Pistols as replacement headliners. So the tour was still on track and selling
tickets.

For this reason, Melinda and Owen had decided to stay on and catch shows in Cincinnati, Pittsburgh, Buffalo, and Boston before heading home to get ready for college.

When I spoke to Melinda on the phone, she was excited about seeing Britain's punk pioneers, but also worried about me, my lack of prospects, and my general depression.

"You've got to talk to Borman," she urged. "It's too late for him to hurt Owen. So get down on your knees and beg him to clean up your record."

"What for?" I grumbled. "I'll never get my scholarship back. I'm sure they awarded it to somebody else."

"Maybe so," she argued. "But there's always next year, and the year after that. A black mark like cheating could hold you back for the rest of your life."

"Who's the Young Republican now?" I teased her.

"Do it, Leo. Don't screw around. It's important."

The one bright spot in all this was that Melinda and I had agreed to try a long-distance relationship this new school year, despite our religious differences—goth and Republican.

I couldn't resist visiting Graffiti-Wall.usa for the occasional glimpse into my new girlfriend's virtual soul. This was what KafkaDreams had to say about me: nothing. Not one word.

Which didn't necessarily mean I had no effect at all on Melinda's online world.

DarthLightning03:

> what happened to u, kd? the edge is gone,
> the attitude, the ability to spot the bs and
> blast it out of the water—if I want sunshine
> and roses, i'll log onto barney. u don't even
> suck anymore. . . .

CzechBouncer was even more to the point:

> Americans always desert you in the end. I'm
> going to download free music and it's on your
> head. . . .

Of course the change in Melinda might not have been me at all. It might have had something to do with the absence of makeup, hair dye, and several pounds of flowing gothica.

"It's all going straight back on the minute I've got regular access to a decent bathroom," she had assured me. "Accept me the way I am or not at all."

And I caved. Of course I caved! I'd never really

had the guts to stand up to Melinda. Why should now be any different?

Yet looking at the postings on Graffiti-Wall, I wasn't so sure she'd be going all-goth again. Partway, yes. She had her style—that was one of the great things about her. But I sensed a subtle softening of the granite exterior of the immortal KafkaDreams. I like to think I had something to do with that.

Melinda was *happy*.

If only I could say the same for myself.

Mr. Borman scheduled office hours starting two weeks before the opening of school. Somehow, the prospect of sitting opposite this man did little to improve my mood. I secured an appointment for the first available afternoon.

Home was like a split-level Crock-Pot where a guy could stew in his own misery. After the initial shock of seeing me walk off the plane not dead, Mom was pretending I'd never been gone, and certainly not with King Maggot. Obviously, denial is a river in Egypt for this woman.

Or maybe not. There was something she said, hunting for a puzzle piece—one puzzle, not an entire houseful of them. "Comes a time," she mumbled, "that you just have to stop apologizing."

I put my hand on hers, covering part of a Stonehenge monolith. "You're right, Mom." McMurphy—the worst McMurphy—would be a part of me forever. But at a certain point, that had to be *my* problem. Mom's penance was over. She had done her time.

There was no way I would ever tell her that the watershed trauma in her life had not been King, but his sex-maniac cousin. The poor woman had spent nearly twenty years coming to terms with her brief liaison with a rock star. If she had to scale that back to a sleazy womanizing manager, I couldn't predict how she'd take it.

Dad's opinion: "I'm just happy I can walk in my own home without stepping on the Hanging Gardens of Babylon." But his next comment, five minutes home from the airport, was the forty-thousand-dollar question. "So? Are we going to Harvard?"

"No."

"He turned you down?"

"I didn't ask. You were right. It was a lousy thing to do."

He looked unhappy. "Your dorm assignment came in the mail. I hope it's not too late to get our deposit back. We can put it in the account I've set up for next year."

"Thanks, Dad," I said, and meant it. But the truth was, next year may as well have been fifteen centuries in the future. The here and now looked like a hardware store job, weekend trips to see Melinda, and a whole lot of woulda, shoulda, coulda.

East Brickfield Township High School. A couple of months ago, I'd been a student here. Now the place was as alien and remote as a moonscape. Worse than that, because of the circumstances of my graduation, it felt hostile.

The walls began to close in on me as I approached the assistant principal's office. This was enemy territory. In a campground outside Boston, I knew Melinda and Owen were sending me psychic energy. I wished I could have taken Owen out of that equation. He was a great guy, but he had an unpleasant knack for turning everything he touched into doo-doo. On the other hand, he couldn't hurt me much now. How much lower can you go than rock bottom? Unless Borman had hired Detective Sergeant Ogrodnick to help at the meeting. . . .

They were cutting the grass outside the office. So every few minutes we had to shut up and wait for a guy on a John Deere riding mower to roar past the picture window. It made an awkward con-versation even more so.

"How was your summer, Leo?"

Looking at Borman, I realized that I didn't want to beg; I wanted to hit him. It was McMurphy, I knew. But this time my hitch-hiker wasn't some stranger. *I* was McMurphy, and McMurphy was me.

"Not bad," I replied. "I guess you've heard that I won't be going to Harvard."

To his credit, he didn't grin. "I was sorry about that. Still, it was your decision."

McMurphy wanted to say, *No, it was your deci-sion, you sick fascist.* But that wasn't exactly in keep-ing with the goals of this appointment. I had to suck it up and be polite.

"Mr. Borman, what I came to talk about is this: it's too late for this year. But I need you to take that black mark off my record. I'm never going to get into a decent school if people think I'm a cheater. And you know I'm not."

It would have been easy for him. All he would have had to say was okay.

He didn't. "Part of being an educator, Leo, is to teach students that actions have consequences."

"What actions?" I countered, my voice rising in volume as the mower approached again. "Refusing to help you crucify a kid because you don't like his lifestyle? You know I didn't cheat."

He waited for the grass cutter to pass. At last, in a quiet, stubborn voice, he said, "You broke the rules."

"I did. I talked during a test. Isn't this kind of a steep price to pay for that?"

I looked longingly outside at blue sky and scudding white clouds. It was a beautiful day. What was I doing in here, beating my head against a stone wall, looking for mercy from someone who had none to give? "This has nothing to do with consequences," I went on resentfully. "You won't clear my record because that would be admitting you were in the wrong from the start. To you, this is all about saving face."

He was angry now. "Exactly who do you think you're talking to—?"

The engine noise swelled again, drowning him out. He stood up to wave the grass cutter away to another part of the lawn, and then cried out in shock. His leap across the office would have won an Olympic medal in several different categories.

All at once, I saw what he saw. For a nanosecond, a dark shadow eclipsed the light from outside. The next thing I knew, the window exploded, and a half-ton of screaming metal machinery was hurtling into Borman's office in a blizzard of broken glass.

The gleaming Harley-Davidson hit the office floor, skidded in a half-circle, and stalled out. So help me, I thought the rider was dead. But he rose from the wreckage and shook himself like a wet dog, spraying glass everywhere.

The one and only Marion X. McMurphy.

King Maggot turned punk rock's most storied rage on the assistant principal of East Brickfield Township High.

"You call yourself a teacher! Is it a teacher's job to keep great kids out of Ivy League schools? I'd puke on you, but that would be a waste of good puke!"

Borman recovered enough to rasp, "You're in big trouble, mister!"

King seemed impatient. "Just remember that if it happens to me, it goes on page one—right beside the story of the piece-of-crap principal who tried to ruin a student's life!"

"You're insane!" Borman hissed.

"Damn right," King agreed. He took a single threatening step toward the assistant principal.

Borman scrambled to his feet and out the door. We could hear his running footsteps tearing down the hall. I have to say that almost made the whole thing worth it—the sight of my archenemy high-tailing it out of his own office in fear for his life.

But there were more urgent issues at hand.

"King, what are you doing here? How did you find me? How did you know I'd be meeting Borman right now?"

"Your friend Owen told me."

"Owen is in Boston with Concussed!" I persisted. "How could he find you in California?"

"Cam knows my number. He signed on with Pete and the Stem Cells after we dropped off the tour."

"Cam?" Was I missing something here? What did my ex-roommate and tormentor have to do with Owen Stevenson?

"Didn't you know? Owen and Cam are together now."

"Together?" When Owen told us he'd met someone, he was talking about *Cam*?

I was floored. I thought back to the heaps of abuse Cam had laid on me for holding him back from picking up girls. To hear him talk, you'd have thought he was Bernie in training. And all this time he was *gay*?

It was crazy—yet the more I thought about it, the more it made perfect sense.

How pleasant could it have been for Cam to

hide his true identity in the sexually charged macho world of rock and roll? No wonder the guy was in a bad mood all the time. I should have suspected something when Owen came up with a backstage pass in Cleveland, and it hadn't come from me.

Owen and Cam together? Good for them!

King glared at me. "Where do you get off not telling me you lost your scholarship because of this jerk?"

"It wasn't your problem."

"Don't you get it?" he snapped at me. "Your problem *is* my problem. Why do you think I flew three thousand miles to crash this meeting? My samurai sword got confiscated by airport security. And you think you can rent a Harley just anywhere? I was all over Connecticut looking for this thing—which I'll have to pay to fix!" He flipped up his shades and skewered me with those piercing eyes. "That's a stiff tab when you add in tuition for Harvard."

I stared at him—this rock star standing in the wreckage of Borman's office, glittering with glass splinters, bleeding from a thousand tiny cuts. I realized that my first impression of him had been one-hundred-percent correct. He was a maniac. And yet he had just offered to do the finest thing anyone had ever done for me.

"King—I can't let you pay for me. The truth is, you're not my father. Bernie is."

It was painfully hard to say, but once it was out, I knew it was right.

I thought he'd be shocked, but he shrugged it off with an impatient gesture. "Oh, I figured that."

I gawked at him.

"Listen, Leo, I was no saint during the eighties, but I remember me, and I remember Bernie. I always knew there was a chance it might be him you were looking for."

"I wish it wasn't true," I said fervently.

"It's a technicality," he insisted. "We're still family. I knew the night we kidnapped the wrong mutt that I didn't give a damn if the DNA test didn't go our way. I want to be a part of your life."

"King—" I stumbled forward to embrace him, but he warded me off with a stiff-arm.

"No offense, Leo, but I'm in a lot of pain right now."

I was worried. "I'll take you to the hospital."

"The cops'll be here soon," he commented blithely. "They'll look after me."

As if on cue, we heard sirens approaching.

He was three thousand miles from home, battered and bleeding, about to be arrested. Yet I'd never seen him so serene. I recalled a comment he'd made about the first Harley incident: *If something came along that was really worth caring about, I could get just as worked up as I used to in the eighties.*

King Maggot cared that much about *me*.

I turned to him. "What can I do for you? How can I help?"

"You can get out of here," he replied. "Go home and start packing. Freshman orientation starts in a week."

We could see the cops now through what was left of the window—two squad cars turning up the drive.

"But I want to help *you*!"

"Okay," he agreed. "You know the drill. Call Bernie—he's still my personal manager. He'll get the lawyers, set up bail—the usual. Now, scram!"

And I did, sprinting through the school and exiting via the fire doors in the gym. Leo Caraway, former Young Republican, soon of Harvard, escaping in full flight, just a few steps ahead of the police. I should have been beside myself, terrified, close to hysterics. Instead, I was strangely calm as I scrambled into my mother's car and gunned the engine.

We McMurphys know how to act in a crisis.